The Nights

Helen Hopcroft

SPINELESS WONDERS
PO Box 220
Strawberry Hills
NSW Australia 2012
shortaustralianstories.com.au
First published by Spineless Wonders 2024

Printed and bound by Fast Proof Press
Distributed by NewSouth Books through Alliance
Distribution Services
ISBN 978-0-6483988-5-1

The Nights

Helen Hopcroft

Contents

Foreword
Written By Carmel Bird

Scheherazade, the woman who tells tales, spins yarns to save her life, is one of the most fascinating figures in literature's galaxy of narrators. If she can keep the Sultan interested in her stories as well as her body, she will not be executed. Suspense is the key. Keep him waiting for the happy resolution. Tale tumbles into tale. She mesmerises the Sultan for a thousand and one nights, escapes alive, and will forever after hold the world as her audience. She stealthily embodies the nexus between a reader's engagement with story and the simple universal fact of sexuality.

Helen Hopcroft is a celebrated visual artist with a highly individual approach to her work. She is also a writer who has studied the fairy tale in great depth. In 2017 she created a living artwork in My Year as a Fairy Tale wherein she spent a year dressed as Marie Antoinette while going about her own regular everyday Australian life.

So perhaps it is no surprise that now, in The Nights, she has adopted the voice of Scheherazade and constructed a life and a collection of tales to form a dazzling insight into the nature of those thousand and one nights. It was sex and it was stories, and here the two have equal roles.

This Scheherazade is frank and brutal in her erotic verbal renderings of the sexual act. She can also be lyrical and seductive in her language, lulling readers with words and images, only to shock them with sudden graphic descriptions of carnality. At one point she explains that in her heart she knows there is no real division between humans and beasts.

Here readers will find a rich and intriguing vein of new tales that echo with the tropes of the familiar Once Upon a Time, but that are swiftly undercut by the personal narrative of the relentless storyteller-woman who is, after all, in the process of saving her own life. She likens the phenomenon of travel to that of gambling, both activities resting on the belief that 'things will soon improve'. Storytelling, also, belongs in that category. Although things can appear to be deteriorating, or going nowhere, surely something good is going to happen soon.

The happy ending is the orgasm – the story and the sex are in the same business. Where the familiar tales usually gloss over the truths of sexual congress, the stories in The Nights are meticulous in their attention to physical detail. Yet it is detail that disappears in a moment, as the text reverts swiftly back into the world where princes and princesses and wolves and peacocks suffer and celebrate and generally weave their own magic.

Once upon a time Helen Hopcroft picked up her pen and boldly produced a collection of erotic fairy tales. Perhaps, as she wrote, she was dressed as Scheherazade. I like to think so.

Lament

Soon the night will come, and to save my life, I must tell another story. I have found that he likes the midnight tales best: stories from the furnace of my erotic imagination. Since coming here, I have found that the wellspring of my libido, usually a neat little fountain of desire, has sprung and disgorged a jet of longing so intense that I sometimes fear for my sanity. Like many people in times of crisis, I have taken refuge in fantasy. I have found that the deeper into my mind I journey, the more lost I become, the greater the likelihood that I will live to see another morning.

I I lie here feeling the earth travelling around the sun, watching the shadows on the wall grow darker and more elongated, the seconds tick like honey dripping off a spoon, sometimes fast and then gradually slower and slower, until it seems as if the night will never come. But it does. Perhaps I close my eyes for an instant and sleep, oh blessed sleep, because when I open them again the night sky is a black square on the white wall, the darkness speckled with a thousand stars. I have forgotten to close a window and on the ledge perches a nightingale. Outside the window is a small courtyard with lemon trees and high peach-coloured walls; I hear the distant gurgling of a marble fountain.

In this box of a room, with its small hard bed, sheets still musty with the smell of the other girls, I have been chased by fear; it has pursued me into the corners of my mind like a giant rat. I have curled as helpless as an unborn child on this bed, terror my blanket, with the world spinning on its axis like a giant toy. At such times I cling to whatever hope I can muster. My mother always taught me that from any experience something must be gained, that one must not walk away from the table of life without knowledge, or wisdom, whatever that is. And so, in the early days, sickened by the cowering fool that I had become, I turned to face the rat. I stared into its cruel yellow eyes, coolly observed its scimitar fangs, breathed in the smoky reek of the beast. To my surprise, the rat came closer, shrank in size, first burying its soft horse head into my arms, then climbing into my lap like an affectionate cat. Finally, it reached up to tug at the hem of my dress like a playful kitten.

People say fear, like pain, comes in waves. But for me terror lurks deep in the ocean of my mind, while I float leaf-like on its surface. I know that if I ever leave this place, I will spend the rest of my life wondering at the creatures now residing in these depths: a pack so dreadful that even in the bright light of day, with an army of powerful warriors behind me, I could never turn to face them.

And yet I know that this torment has been my salvation.

It is ironic that from the day he took me and brought me to this small room, away from the myriad distractions of the everyday, the multiple paths of destiny, I began to recognise my true self. I climbed out of the iron cage of other people's expectations, thrust aside my cloak of respectability, and discovered a strange new voice lurking deep in the pit of my stomach. When he sickens of me, as he has sickened of us all, and they drag me off to be slaughtered like a pig, I will cry out only this one truth: I am an artist.

Night has come.

Footsteps on the spiral staircase leading up to my room, the dull clack of an unmanned lock, his manservant stands before me. 'He is ready for you,' he murmurs. I blush with shame. Over the nights this servant, with his olive skin and black eyes, irises as poignant as a dead star, has crept into my imagination. His form has re-emerged in a thousand guises. Last night, as I lay before the Sultan, my hand gently stroking my clitoris as I invented yet another tale (for his amusement: for my salvation) this man was the raw meat churning in the mincer of my mind. I have woven him into

I have woven him into many stories, he has fathered many characters; the scent of his skin animates my speech and perfumes my vocabulary.

many stories, he has fathered many characters; the scent of his skin animates my speech and perfumes my vocabulary. I live at the nexus between word and skin. Since coming here, my skin always smells of lilies, and the cleft between my legs remains wet as the earth after a spring rain. Most mornings, the sheets are drenched.

However, despite the villagers' ribald predictions, as the Sultan's men dragged me screaming from my mother's house, he has not fucked me. I remain, technically at least, a virgin. I have stroked him until pearls of sweat ran down the sides of his face, his member swollen and hard, veins throbbing a painful pleasure, skin scarlet with desire, a flower aching to open. I have taken his penis into my mouth, sometimes just the spade shaped tip, squashing like a strawberry into the roof of my mouth; sometimes the whole rigid length, so wide and firm and deep that it stretches my lips thin as vomit threatens to gush upwards. But he has not penetrated me, not yet.

Tonight, I stand, adjust my gown, and follow the manservant out of the door. Soon he will lead me into a gorgeous room, a chamber so sumptuous that my whole family could work their entire lives and never pay for a tenth part of the furnishings that so adorn the space. Even with death hanging over me, as ever present as my shadow, I must take time to describe these beautiful things: a silver tray, on which they bring me black coffee and sweetmeats, with little birds engraved around the edges, its surface a highly polished mirror. (After I have eaten and drunk from eggshell thin cups, but before I begin my nightly story, I sometimes turn the mirror on its side and watch myself masturbate. I have found that it aids the imagination).

In the corner of the room, a piece of furniture that I should call a wardrobe but cannot bear to do so. It is vast, taking up all of the wall and most of the ceiling too, a solid black ebony, with a mess of jewelled birds and tiny red flowers veining the dark wood. If you open it, you will find a soft lining of jade green velvet and a hundred costumes, each more outlandish than the next. I am still a virgin, it is true, but even I know that one woman can become a thousand with such props. And what man would ever tire of a thousand women? Such strategies keep me alive and besides, I like the feeling of fur and raw silk against my naked skin, the inventiveness that such costumes bring to the mind. I have learned that a silk shift, pale and transparent as a cloud, rubbed with the oils from the room's many chests, makes him groan more than usual.

Did I forget to mention that the room is a bedroom? In the centre of the stone floor, a canopied bed as large as a living room, with sheets that I write the story of my life on, blank as the pages of a book. The white cotton stained with body fluids: blood, sweat, semen, shit, stringy pieces of globular snot, tears, urine, hot spit, my own jellyfish come. Lately I have taken to tangling myself up in the pale muslin curtains gracing the sides of the bed, and sometimes they rip, but I find that he likes this too. More than once, he has unwrapped me from the shredded pieces of feather light fabric, hands urgent with need, penis straining against his silk shorts, seams forced apart by his need.

But hush, now it's story time, and like the nightingale, I must sing for the darkness.

The Woman Who was Sick of Her Husband

There was once a woman who married her childhood sweetheart and remained true to him. She remained faithful even when her husband left her alone for months and then years at a time. This was no easy matter, for he was a trader whose caravan wandered through the deserts of the south, the tundras of the north. And Margareta, for that was the wife's name, was a woman with breasts like ripe peaches, a river of black hair and skin as white as wildflower seed. When she was a girl she would run through her village, hair a flickering black flag, dark eyes burning like the smouldering coals of a winter fire. Fifty years have passed since then, and people still speak of this girl as if she lives now and will run through the village at any moment.

Somehow time passed and, as everyone knows, time moves slower in the desert than anywhere else in the world. While her husband's caravan wandered through the endless mountains of sand, Margareta grew old. She bore her husband three sons and, as is the way of the world, they all left her to find their fortunes and never returned. It's not that they didn't love their mother, rather their love was so profound that the three boys needed no reassurance of its existence. Perhaps if Margareta had given birth to a daughter, things would have been different, but as it was, she mourned alone in her little house under the date palms. Slowly her long black hair turned grey, like snow falling over basalt in winter, and her skin became icy, so infrequently was her husband at home.

In their middle years, Margareta's husband sold his caravan, fearing the barbarians to the north, and the flood of cheap imported goods to the south. He brought his chest of gold home with him and left his camels tethered to the date palms. Every day he would sit in the back garden, eating dates and looking at the birds fluttering in the trees. He would not move, except to begin some small job, which he never finished, and he would not enter the house, except for meals and to sleep. Margareta knew that when her husband stared up at the sky, he was seeing the blazing clouds of a desert storm, and when he sat at her table, he was thinking longingly of a meal eaten cross-legged on the sand of the desert floor.

Margareta was a proud woman who had not forgotten the beauty of her youth. She looked in the mirror and saw lines dragging down the sides of her mouth; privately she described these as her 'marriage lines'. She held up her once dove-like hands, now work hardened claws, and this burning stone of a woman wept. She caressed her magnificent breasts, as soft as fledgling swans, and bitterly counted the nights since her husband had nestled his face in their scented crevice. After ten nights she was angry and disappointed; when ten stretched to thirty her moods were so intolerable that the last remaining household servant packed his bags and left; and by the time one hundred nights had passed, Margareta was as intractable as a granite boulder. When it became apparent that without assistance her husband would continue to sigh as he looked up into the sky, and weep as he looked down at the sand, she tied on her blackest veil and went to consult the wise woman.

Now the wise woman lived in a little hovel on the edge of the village, and while at some time or another most villagers had consulted her, no one would openly admit to it. As a source of advice, she was publicly scorned, privately revered. When a woman in the village had a problem that none of the other women could solve, they would float discrete hands across their mouths and whisper, in rustling voices soft as a bird preening its feathers, 'Only the wise woman can help you'. Over the years the richest and the poorest had found themselves at the wise woman's door. She treated all alike, sending them back into the world with the golden gift of peace in their hearts: such was the immaculate healing power of the old woman.

Margareta waited for the sun to set before leaving her little house under the date palms. Silently she crept through the village, timidly examining every shadow, wringing her hands with worry. It was midnight before she knocked at the wise woman's door. The noise disturbed a large owl sleeping on the lintel. Margareta cried out in alarm as a feathered shape flew straight at her face, veering away at the last second, curved claws inches from her eyes. Unnerved, she was about to turn and run when two things happened: a strong, kind voice called out, 'Come in'. And the force of the hundred nights suddenly overwhelmed her, swooping into her mind like a large bird. She thought of the many nights she had lain in bed, legs parted with longing, while her husband slept indifferent on the far side of the mattress, a tundra of space between them. She gathered her cloak around her, for it was a cold night, and summoning her courage, entered the house. Like all desperate wives, she prepared to break the ultimate female taboo and tell the truth about her marriage.

First one hour passed, and the owl returned to snooze once again on the wooden lintel, tucking shining golden eyes beneath a striped wing. Then two hours passed; stars whirled and exploded across the night sky, while fat bats returned from their evening hunt. When three hours passed, the night air became heavy with sighs as souls left their dead bodies and floated up towards heaven; for, as any nurse can tell you, the hour before dawn is the time that the old and the sick mostly choose to die. After four long hours had passed, and the black night had faded to the blue of an old bruise, and all the stars had gone home to bed, Margareta finally emerged from the old woman's house. The owl watched her thank its inhabitant in a voice sugar sweet with gratitude, and as she walked away, a curious little smile twitched at the corners of her mouth. The owl had only seen this woman briefly, when she bashed on the door, disturbing his evening nap, but she seemed much changed. Although it was still dark, he could have sworn that beneath her long robe, curvaceous hips were moving with the swaying curls of a desert python.

What passed between the two women that night remains a secret, and the new day dawned pretty much as any other. Margareta's husband stared at the sky, longing for the desert, and scornfully regarded the walls of the house, wishing them somehow transformed into the canvas of a nomad's tent. While Margareta felt new knowledge boil inside her, outside the day dragged past like a slow dripping tap. Breakfast was eaten as the sun rose, lunch was served in the glare of midday light, and after an endless afternoon, when even the birds got sick of singing, the sun finally dropped low in the sky. Margareta bustled about, intent on her chores, while outside her husband looked up at the sky and sighed, wept as he looked down at the ground. Night arrived like ink slowly staining the sky black. In the east, the first stars began to twinkle in the dusk.

Wondering at the lateness of the hour, Margareta's husband waited for her to call him inside for dinner. He waited until the plum-coloured shadows of the palm trees stretched up in the sky and became the same blue as the night. He waited until the nightingales began their evening dance, swooping low overhead, their long tail feathers brushing against his hair. And he waited as the orange jasmine vine puffed out its deliriously sweet nocturnal perfume. It wasn't until his stomach began to growl like an angry lion that he stood up, mechanically brushed the legs of his trousers with his hands, and slowly walked inside, bones stiff with the evening damp. Mentally he composed a speech with which to chastise his wife, 'How late was his dinner!' But as he walked inside, he found that he was actually enjoying being angry: it was a nice change from being sad.

His wife wasn't there. A strange woman was bent over at the stove, her large bottom standing out like an enormous peach, the velvet ribbon of a long blonde plait hanging down the centre of her spine. The delicious smell of roasting lamb, baked vegetables and bitter chocolate filled the small room. Startled, he cleared

his throat, taking a step backwards. When the woman turned to face him, Margareta's husband cried out in shock: it was his wife! His wife, transformed by a thousand small changes: a dress that plunged below the deep valley of her breasts, a platinum blonde wig, jewels sparkling like a sharp frost on the dappled flesh of her upper arms. The man drew in a sharp breath of desire and puffed out another of frustration. 'What are you doing, Margareta?' he demanded. 'You must have spent hours dressing yourself so, while your husband goes hungry. Shame on you, woman!'

Margareta smiled at him. The smile of an angry goddess, a smile to crack rocks on a barren hillside, a smile to scorch the sun and freeze the moon from the sky. Her husband took another step back, suddenly fearful of this changed personage. 'I am not Margareta,' his wife announced politely, her lips clearly rolling each syllable. 'Tonight, I am Roxanne, and you will address me as such.' She reached behind her and pulled a steaming dish of good food off the oven top. Looking her husband straight in the eye, she hurled the dish down onto the kitchen floor, smashing it into a thousand pieces. Like a dormant volcano, she suddenly exploded into life, roaring in a red voice, 'And you can get your own damned dinner!'

Her husband surged forward, eyes full of fear, but with an arm raised to deliver a punishing blow. Margareta stepped forward, calm as a cowherd tending her flock, stopped him with one meaty forearm, gathered his waist in an iron grip and slammed his body down onto the floor. With deadly accuracy she ripped off his clothes as he squirmed helpless on the food-smeared tiles. Pinning him down with her gigantic breasts, for he was but a small man, she scooped a chunk of lamb fat off the floor and reaching for his penis, quickly brought it to an oily zeal. Her hand moving so fast that it made a clicking sound, Margareta's husband gasped like a drowning man, sweat pouring from his brown forehead like water. His legs kicked a drumbeat against the kitchen floor, muscles spasming with the intensity of his pleasure.

Margareta climbed on top, rammed his penis into the waiting cleft of her soaking vagina and pounded away like a hammer striking stone. Underneath his massive wife, the little man arched and writhed in ecstasy, fingers clenching the rippled fat of her pearly thighs as over and over he called out her name, 'Margareta! Margareta!' When his orgasm came, the force lifting him off the floor like a fish jerking on a line, he screamed it again: 'Margareta!' But his wife merely stuck her oily little finger into his anus, increasing his frantic howls of desire, and coolly repeated her new name. 'Tonight, I am Roxanne.'

After that night, things were different in the little house under the date palms. Margareta instructed her husband to buy another caravan, and he obediently did so, reverting to his former life of travelling for months and returning for weeks. But this time, whenever he came home, a new woman greeted him. Sometimes a red-headed Roxanne would rush down the path of their house, push him breathless and shaking to the ground, the gravel grinding into her fat knees as she took him where he lay. Once a raven-haired beauty, resplendent in tanned black cow hide, deeply and bloodily scored his back. And sometimes she was a ravenously blonde. He would walk nervously into his own house, never knowing what to expect: a demure innocent with wide eyes and powder-soft hands, or the fury that had

attacked with such savagery on the night Roxanne was born. The husband knew that all these women were Margareta, and she was all of them. He saw no hypocrisy in her play-acting, only a splendid new kind of freedom, blessed with the same hunger with which men made war.

Margareta's husband would cross deserts where a thousand miles was reckoned a short distance, pitch his tent and gaze up at the everlasting stars. He would listen to the sound of sandstorms rushing in waves across the limitless space. The man would rise at dawn, travel nomads' highways until dusk, rocked to sleep on the swaying back of his camel, pausing only to cook his evening meal over a campfire, a small speck of light in a whole world of darkness. And whenever he stopped to rest, he looked into the heart of the fire, and he thought of his wife.

Suckle

I slept for a long time. When I wake it is late afternoon, with the sound and smells of the city's market drifting in the window. I smell fresh cinnamon, nutmeg, star anise, the icy green scent of papaya, sickly-sweet waft of mango, warm comfort of rotten bananas. I imagine wicker baskets heaped with ripe figs, seeds bursting from their swollen sides, piles of limp greens heaped on the hot ground, and animals tethered in the shade of the palm trees. Under the cover of canvas tents, at the edge of the market, dozens of tethered camels, horses, monkeys, rancid goats and thin sheep will change owners. Of all the thousands of lies told in a market, falsities more infinite than the stars above, most are told in the stench of the animal tents.

Someone has crept into my room while I slept and left a large bowl of fruit on the table. Such delicacies! I wander over and choose a firm mango, bashing it against the stone tabletop as my mother once showed me, until the flesh has liquefied and the skin is tender thin with bruises. Taking a silver knife, I cut a tiny cross into one plump side, licking the sweet sap that oozes from the cut. Reclining on the bed, I raise the cut to my mouth and suck, squeezing the mango with my hands. Smashed flesh trickles into my waiting mouth as I use my fingers to pump the mango's sides. When the giant fruit is dry, and all that remains is the empty bladder of the skin – clinging lecherously to its furry pip – I lick the last juice from my fingers.

Last night, while I was telling my story, I noticed the Sultan looking at me with a new expression on his face. It was a look that I cannot describe, and like all those whose life lies precariously balanced on the whim of another, this troubles me. Sometimes when I look into his eyes it is like standing on a mountain on a clear summer's day: I can see as far as it is possible to see, nothing is hidden from me, he has no secrets. On other evenings, like last night, I look into his eyes and there is nothing. No vestige of emotion, no humour, no understanding, no trace of human feeling. This is a man who has seduced scores of young women, enjoyed their pleasures, ravaged their bodies, and then in the morning destroyed them as if they were no more than insects. All lovely young women, radiant with their first glow of life. All girls just like me.

The hour is getting late. I watch shadows creep up the walls, feel the first stirrings of the evening breeze animate the tepid air, while I sit here struggling to invent a new story with which to regale him. I need a fresh narrative, something so enthralling that it will keep me alive another night, a story that is beautiful or intriguing or funny or wise. Yet somehow that strange look in his eyes has frozen the part of my mind I need for this task. My imagination is dead, my creative mind a locked door. I am no more capable of inventing a story than I am of flying like a bird, running on all fours like a horse, or even swimming like a fish.

I ponder the tremendous release of swimming in deep, cool water. To be submerged and yet still to breathe, the freedom of a silver-skinned creature to swivel its fins and float without weight or care, suspended in liquid. I long to remove this odd feeling of desecration that haunts me, which clings like an oily residue to my skin. I need to wet myself and scrub away every trace of my defilement as if, like dirt, it is something so easily removed. I think longingly of his marble bath, milky water flowing through golden swan-shaped taps, warm liquid swirling through my hair and caressing my long legs. I remember running the taps so that a thin trickle of water descended to tickle my clitoris. I burn with an aching need, an overwhelming desire, to be clean. I have stayed alive, it is true, but every single morning I count the cost, and the price is greater each day.

We are made of stories, and having sold my own collection to cheat death, I find that I have none left for myself.

We are made of stories, and having sold my own collection to cheat death, I find that I have none left for myself. The only story I cannot tell is my own, for I do not know how it ends; yet I realise, with something like sadness, that there is no other person in this world who can tell it for me. Like an animal living in a cage, a refugee without a country, my destiny remains an unfinished tale.

The Storyseller

In the oasis of time before sunset, I leaf through the small supply of books that the manservant has left by my bed. It is an odd collection - I wonder where he finds them - comprising of children's picture books, dusty tomes of epic poetry, and seemingly true accounts of rugged desert journeys. As the sky darkens, and the nightingale's chorus builds, I choose a book at random. There is no writing on the spine or cover, so I unfurl the scarlet leather binding and begin to flick through the heavy cream pages. It seems as if this book has been lovingly prepared: the pages include many fine black-and-white line drawings, every colourful illustration looks hand-painted.

There was once an old man who sold stories, just like a baker sells bread or a butcher sells meat or a cobbler sells shoes. Every morning the old man would rise at dawn, stretch his rickety limbs, and breakfast on a simple meal of grilled goat's cheese and salted honey. Then he'd ride towards the city market on a grey donkey with a halo of flies buzzing slowly around its shaggy head. The man and his donkey were so ancient that the journey always took them a very, very long time. Each morning, they left the cottage shortly before sunrise so as to arrive by lunch.

Arriving at the market, the man would find himself a nice quiet spot near the wine merchants and set up a humble stall. The stall consisted of a piece of sun-bleached ship's timber balanced between two wooden crates, with an old piece of orange silk thrown over the top. The silk must have once been a beautiful piece of

material – you could still see the faded remnants of embroidered finches on it – and its colour seemed to draw people towards the stall. And the timber must have once been part of a powerful vessel, for on one wide plank were some finely carved letters – N E M A – all that remained of the ship's former glory.

From midday until dusk, the old man sat behind his stall, selling original stories for a few coins to passers-by. In between customers, he shared endless cups of black tea and local gossip with the neighbouring wine merchants. Every day was both the same as the last, and completely different, for the old man had a never-ending supply of stories that he mixed into new forms for each customer. Although dusty and poor, with worn out boots and a much-darned coat, the storyseller was a master of his craft. He told fantastic stories about treasure and fierce dragons, homely tales of love and marriage, epic fantasies of seduction and revenge, tragic sagas about lost children and missing fortunes, charming anecdotes that blended real life with dreams, and even composed lyrical verse for special occasions such as birthdays or weddings. Having purchased a story, many people would return to the old man again and again over the years, so he had a steady stream of old customers and new.

One day, shortly after midday, a tall man strode over to the old man's stall. He was a soldier, an older man with blonde hair and green eyes, armed with a razor-sharp scimitar, and wearing the gorgeous livery of the Sultan's private guard. Fearing the worst, the storyseller immediately straightened up – perhaps he had offended a powerful person in some way! – but the soldier smiled at him good-naturedly. 'I'd like to buy a story for my betrothed,' said the man. 'We're about to get married and are keen to start a family: I hope to have a daughter, she longs for a son. Regardless, I'd like a good story to share with her on our wedding night.'

The storyseller sighed with relief. 'Yes,' he said, 'I'm sure I have the perfect story for such an occasion. What is your future wife's name?'

'Nadine', said the soldier.

'And what does she look like?', asked the old man.

'She has flame-coloured hair and eyes which are exactly the colour of a winter sky before snow. She is the most beautiful woman I have ever seen, and I love her with all my heart'.

The storyseller crafted the soldier a fine tale, about a lovely woman with red hair and winter-coloured eyes who marries a powerful king, and the soldier left him with many grateful thanks and a golden coin.

A few weeks later, the soldier returned to the old man's stall. This time there was no cheerful greeting, no welcoming smile. The soldier staggered as he lurched against the piece of ship's timber, sending the sunset-coloured silk tumbling down into the dirt. His green eyes were blank with shock and his skin was deathly pale.

'What happened?', asked the storyseller, aghast. 'Didn't she like the story?'

'She didn't get to hear it', said the soldier, breathing heavily. He collapsed onto a small wooden crate that the old man used as a stool. 'On the night before our wedding, the Sultan sent for her, demanded that she marry him instead. I tried to hide her but they dragged her from the house. She is his wife now.'

'I'm so sorry,' said the old man, gesturing to one of the nearby merchants, who scurried over with a carafe of red wine. The soldier gulped the wine down as if it was water, and the storyseller quickly refilled his cup. It was a long time before the man was able to speak.

'Nadine came to the palace to visit me,' said the soldier, wiping his eyes. 'She wanted to show me a dress she had picked out for the wedding: just a white cotton thing, but very becoming with her red hair. She was waiting for me outside, in the courtyard with the lemon trees, wearing her white dress with her long hair hanging down. And then the Sultan saw her ...'

The old man waited patiently for the soldier to finish weeping. 'Son,' he murmured, 'what can I do to ease your burden?'

'Your story!' cried the soldier, suddenly ferocious. 'I'm certain that your story caused this! And now I want you to sell me another story, one in which Nadine is no longer married to the Sultan, but instead finds eternal happiness with her true love.'

'Certainly', said the old man, stroking his chin thoughtfully. And he told another wonderful tale, about a passionate red-haired woman who found both her true love and freedom from her powerful husband. By the end of the story, the soldier was sobbing with delight. He picked up the piece of silk, dusted it off, and laid two gold coins on the ship's timber.

A month passed, and the old man continued his early morning journeys to the market on his fly-speckled donkey. One morning, much to his surprise, he found the blonde soldier waiting for him. The man's face was flushed scarlet, and he was so enraged that he could barely breathe. 'What happened?' stammered the old man. 'I sold you a good story – it had everything you asked for in it.'

'Yes,' said the soldier grimly, gritting his teeth. 'Your story certainly did its work. Nadine did find true love, and she is no longer married to the Sultan; that much is true.'

'Then what's the problem?' asked the storyseller, face twitching with concern.

'She didn't find true love with me!' shouted the soldier. 'She found it with a palace servant. For the last month, they've been all over each other like snakes, taking crazy risks, and yesterday the Sultan caught them making love in the palace gardens.' A single tear trickled its way down the man's reddened cheek. 'He cut off their heads,' he finished in a flat voice. And then he laid his head down on the old piece of ship's timber and sobbed like a child.

'Oh dear,' said the storyseller, 'oh dear, oh dear, oh dear.'

For a man whose job it was to craft words, the story-seller suddenly found himself in notably short supply. He gestured to the wine merchant for two large carafes and sat there drinking with the bereaved man. Time passed as they wordlessly emptied glass after glass. Finally, the old man broke the silence. 'What would you like me to do?' he asked.

The soldier looked at him with the unwavering stare of a hunting dog. 'I want you to sell me one more story,' he replied. Looking around, the soldier lowered his voice, and with desperate fingers leant forward and clutched the old man's wrist. 'For a thousand nights, I want the

Sultan to find no solace in a woman's embrace. I want him to feel no pity, no joy, and no fear. I want him to forget what it means to be human.' The man leaned even closer and hissed in the old man's ear: 'I want the beast to eat his heart.' And with that, the soldier stood up, laid a pile of gold coins and a scrap of white cotton on the humble stall, nodded respectfully at the storyseller and walked away. The old man took a deep breath, looked imploringly at the sky, and began telling this story, about an old man who sold a story to a blonde soldier with green eyes.

Bathe

'Come here', I instruct the Sultan, 'I have something I want you to do for me'. He nods, silent tonight, his black eyes still opaque. A powerful man, straight-backed with a broad chest, hair curls across his torso in fine dark waves. I have sucked, bitten and licked every inch of his body. While the hair on his chest grows in shell-like waves, the stuff of his pubis strands and distorts with the flowing movement of a sea anemone. On his legs, rigid shafts of fine black wire, similar to the sharp buzz of his cheeks and chin. I like sliding my cunt over his chin, the sand-paper feel of his strong jaw chewing into my wet-ness. I sometimes let myself move over his mouth, his tongue catching in my groove and flicking up into the dark sun of my anus, but not tonight. This evening I want to be cleaned by the man whose violence has so defiled me.

'I am going to run a bath,' I tell him, 'and when I call you, I want you to come into the bathroom and wash me.' At this his black eyes glitter. I know he likes my skin best when it is wet, many nights we have slipped and slid against each other like playful seals. I lower my eyes, not wanting him to see my contempt, and am greeted by the sight of his penis twitching in readiness beneath his silky robe. Seeing this longed-for organ quivering with anticipation, semi-erect and pulsing with life, brings a hot jet of saliva into my mouth. I stamp on this feeling as if grinding fire ants underfoot. Power runs coldly through my blood, freezing my mind, allowing me to enjoy my control over him; it is the only authority I possess.

I turn and slowly walk away from him, feeling his eyes burn into my spine, then flick downwards to caress the hem of my short shift. This garment is carefully chosen. While opaque, it reaches just below my naked buttocks, and if I should bend ever so slightly over, it rides up to reveal the twin mounds of my vulva. I like the way it looks. Earlier this evening, I watched myself in a mirror, seeing exactly how far I could tilt forward before the shift lifted enough to reveal my sex.

Ruefully, as I regarded my reflection, I found myself wanting him to be there. I imagined him standing behind me, looking at me in the mirror, rough hands delicately lifting the shift slowly up and then bending me forward like a deck of paper cards. I pictured him wetting his fingers in his mouth, his beautiful mouth, with lips that flare and curve like a woman's. And plunging those fingers deep into me from behind, curling them up to caress the roof of my cervix, rhythmic plunges, stroking slow and deep, until I am wet and slippery with desire.

Impatient for the night to come and feeling the cruel need to inflict my subjugation on another, I chose to summon his manservant into my room. He came and stood there, alone, large dark eyes, slim and bronze-skinned, graceful as a young gazelle. 'The Sultan will send for me soon,' I informed the servant, speaking in the voice that had so infuriated the boys in my village. Lifting my chin and pretending self-importance, I added, 'And it is vital that he finds me appealing. I want

you to tell me what you think of this dress.' I twirled in front of him, approached the boy, allowing the silky stuff to ride up over my thighs. 'Does it become me?' I whispered, suddenly vulnerable, coming closer still. Obviously embarrassed, he tried to look away, and I noticed him choke down a mouthful of fresh saliva. 'Look at me,' I commanded, pushing the side of his jaw with my palm and forcing him to face me. I walked over towards the mirror, his eyes locked on me as if by chains, then slowly bent forward until my forehead touched the cool mercury surface of the reflective glass. Over my shoulder, I casually asked him, 'Do you think it is too short?' When he did not answer, I spread my legs.

But now it is night, and I am filling the Sultan's marble bath; the water is scented with gardenias. It is almost as if he has foreseen my desire: the room is speckled with white blooms, their elusive perfume floating through the air in waves, dead waxy petals crumbling underfoot. I fill the bath and then stand looking at the water. I find I am trembling with need, and again squash this horrifying weakness, forcing my voice to be strong as I call out, 'You may come in now.'

I want him, & again I push it back, & down, down to the depths of my mind, to the ocean floor where monsters play.

Suddenly, he is there, quick as a cat, he has moved across the tiled floor silently and fast. I find myself thinking of big cats, the majestic black leopards, screaming lions, animals proud, sexual and stinking of power. I want him, and again I push it back, and down, down to the depths of my mind, to the ocean floor where monsters play. I turn away from him, pulling the shift slowly up over my head, letting it catch on the curved lip of my buttocks, and slide across my pointed breasts. When I finally let the silk fall to the ground, it drifts downwards like smoke. Stepping into the bath, I drop onto all fours, squatting like a dog. I find that I can no longer look at him and that I am shaking. Keeping my voice even I tell him, 'I want you to wash me. I want you to wash me, thoroughly and carefully, as if you were washing an expensive toy. I want you to pretend that I am not a woman, but a thing, some treasure, a prize won in a war. I want you to wash my cunt in the same way you would wash a valuable silver plate: matter of fact, unemotional, thorough. I want to be clean. I want you to clean me.'

And so, he does. He starts at my face with a small cloth, carefully polishing with soap and scented oils, rinsing as he goes, carefully drying with a soft towel. Face, neck, back of neck, chest, breasts. At the breasts, I feel his breathing become deeper and more laboured, a tiny bead of sweat appears in the crease between his eyes, and I sense the heat of his body radiating against my skin. He washes one breast, then another, continuing his careful little circles of soap and oil, moving from the armpit up to the tip. By the time he reaches the nipple it is hard, stiff, and crinkled like a rosebud. He takes a small piece of soap between his thumb and forefinger and delicately pinches the nipple, twisting the soap into the point. A wave of shuddering runs down my back and I feel wet liquid flood my genitals. Then he rinses the nipple with warm water, calmly pats it dry with the towel, and moves onto my arms. 'It was too fast!' I want to cry, my breasts rigid with desire, screaming to be touched.

The feeling of his slow fingers circling down the inside of my arms, brushing the side of my breasts as they descend, pausing to rub the horizontal crease of my elbow, is a kind of torture. I had sworn to myself that I would not respond, but it took all my will to stay still, not to grab his hand and force it into my cunt, not to plunge my breasts into his waiting mouth. The tension in my genitals builds up until it feels like I needed to urinate; an urgent need for orgasm, for release, sending burning fingers of cold pain up and down my back. I push my fingertips and toes into the cool stone of the marble bath and wait for him to finish.

He works methodically, cleaning first my upper back and then my belly and waist, moving back up to wash my buttocks in long, rounded strokes, and then dipping down between my legs to clean there. The same finger and thumb twirl he used on my nipples is repeated on my clitoris and I almost cry out at the bolt of sensation it unleashes. By the time he starts washing my thighs, I get the sense that if I had looked up, I would have seen his sardonic grin. When he finishes, he bows mock-ingly and hands me a towel. He leaves the room before I have the courage to face him. A servant comes and takes me back to my quarters. I stand in my room, a tsunami of disappointment pounding against my chest.

Bird of Paradise

There was once a little girl who wanted a parrot. She begged her parents for a pet bird every day. Each morning, she would come to them with some fresh information about the parrot family's wonderful attributes. 'Parrot feathers are vivid colours,' she would say, 'and so I will learn about art and how to make things pretty.' The next morning, she told them that as the parrot would need to be fed and watered every day, she would 'learn about being responsible and taking care.' Finally, after many days of fascinating parrot facts – each delivered earlier and earlier in the morning – she woke her mother and father up at sunrise with her best argument yet. 'One day my parrot will die,' she said, 'and so I will need to develop courage and resilience.' She was a very clever little girl.

Inevitably, when faced with such resolute persistence, even the strongest armies will crumble. And so it was that the parents succumbed to their daughter's will and purchased her a large macaw from the local market. The macaw came with its own golden cage, a splendid construction that took up a full half of the girl's bedroom. The bird had a salt lick – a chunk of pinkish crystal from the faraway snow-covered mountains – and a simple white china bowl full of water. There was a hessian sack stuffed with sunflower seeds and a bell on a chain, with a little mirror clamped to the side, in case her new pet should become bored. The girl was very, very happy. She named the parrot Egbert.

Egbert and the little girl enjoyed many happy years together. Macaws can grow to be quite elderly birds, and Egbert had the best of care. Every morning, the girl would refresh his pool of clean drinking water, scrub out his lime-encrusted seed bowl, check that the supply of pink salt was adequate. She would sing to her parrot, taught him how to swear in French and recite epic poetry, and carried him around on her bony shoulder. Together they would dance around her bedroom, the macaw ducking and bobbing his head as the little girl beat out sea shanties on a red wooden drum. They soon became the best of friends.

Time passed and the girl grew into a woman. She was a lovely young person, who dressed in brightly coloured silks, loved to paint and play music, was kind and steadfast in her dealings with those around her. The young woman and her bird were adored by all who met them. Grandparents would smile as she walked through the market, with the elderly Egbert perched on her shoulder, and wish that they had brought their own son or daughter a pet macaw. 'That parrot has raised a fine young lady ', an old woman quipped from behind her market stall, 'she is everything a mother could hope for '. And all the other traders – hard men and women with skin so lined that they needed to screw their hats on – grinned and cried out, 'three cheers for the mighty macaw!'

One morning, the young woman woke to find Egbert lying motionless on the floor of his cage. Aghast, she gathered her feathered friend deep into her arms, stroked his warm feathers as the tickle of his heartbeat finally slowed and stopped, and his poor lifeless body

grew cold. She cried until the sawdust floor of Egbert's cage was soggy as mud, her body wracked with shaking sobs, eyes stinging red. Then she picked up her dear macaw, gathered his beloved wooden drum and little mirror, and buried them under a white rose bush in her parents' garden.

The winter came and the rose bush disappeared under a mound of muddy snow. The girl woke early each day, as she had long since become accustomed to doing, then remembered that there was no need to scrub out the seed bowl or refresh her friend's water. Many tears were shed that winter. Then spring came and the rose bush sent out a few feathery green tendrils, delicate and thin but strong as hope. New growth appeared on the bush, first hard purple knobs, later lush green buds the size of plums. The girl waited impatiently for the first rose to appear.

Early one morning, on a day that dawned as bright and clear as the world's first sunrise, the girl woke and decided to visit Egbert's grave. Pulling on a shapeless brown cardigan, she pushed her feet into woollen slippers and tip-toed across the frozen ground to where the rose bush grew. The last snows had melted, but the air was still icy, and the rosebush looked as if it was covered in silver paint. As the girl watched, the ripe buds unfurled revealing first one bloom and then another and another and another. And every single rose was the tropical hue of a macaw's feathers: sunshine yellow, hibiscus red, lagoon blue, jungle green and cloud white. The young woman smiled and bent to kiss the flowers, and touching soft lips to every vivid bloom, farewelled her beloved companion.

The rosebush became moderately famous and every spring there would be a determined line of artists, poets, neighbours, curious onlookers, lay preachers, botanists, floral arrangers, love-sick maidens, sceptics and interior decorators queuing at her parents' door. One morning a young musician appeared at the house, clad in brightly coloured silks and carrying a red wooden drum. The young woman and the minstrel looked at one another, and although they were strangers, spoke to one another as if they were kin.

'I've come to see the rose bush', said the musician.

'You've taken your time', replied the girl. And together they walked through the bright spring garden, chatting and singing and taking turns to play tunes on the red wooden drum.

Ride

The next morning, I sleep late and wake dazed, watching the pattern of light and shadow creeping across the white stone walls of my cell. It is a humble room, simply furnished with carved wooden furniture and ornate red carpets. By the window stands a pitcher of iced water, always kept cold by an army of soft-voiced servants, an amazing feat in the Arabian sun. One pads in now, a blonde maid with an unremarkable face. She deposits a plate of chilled coconut on my bedside table and drifts out again.

I stretch, luxuriating in the feel of clean cotton against my skin, carefully planning my day as a defence against the anxiety that lives at the base of my throat. I have given up counting the number of days I have been here: I think it is about a thousand. I know that he will keep me alive, and play with me, listen to my stories until he is no longer fascinated. Then I will be as dead as the hundreds of other girls he enjoyed before I came here.

When we heard that the Sultan's men were roaming the countryside, searching for virgins, my mother bustled me inside, her face grey with shock. By the fireplace stood my father, slowly sharpening a sword, his proud face expressionless. We had heard the gossip about the new queen: her infidelity, the Sultan's jealous rage, how the screams of the queen and her lover made birds fall dead from the sky. People said that after he had finished with them, even the crows wouldn't touch their bodies. As more travellers rode in from the desert, bringing with them fresh news, the story shifted and became strange. Sickened by his wife's betrayal, the Sultan took refuge in bitter madness, vowing to never let another woman cuckold him. Out of the palace gate rode a phalanx of his most trusted soldiers, their instructions to bring him a new virgin every night. In the morning she was executed. If she pleased him, or was unusually beautiful, her death was quick. That was his only mercy. Families mourned their missing girls as the country waited for the Sultan's vengeance to exhaust itself. They have waited in vain. A thousand nights have passed, and as many girls died, since he took me from my home.

I have given up counting the number of days I have been here: I think it is about a thousand.

Kidnap!

On the day his horsemen rode into my village, I was standing by the well wearing my oldest clothes. My hair had been cut ragged and short, like a boy's, by my father's sword. My face was smeared with soot, I had bare feet, and my teeth were stained with a yellow dye obtained by boiling onion skins (a suggestion of my dear, practical mother). Hearing the sound of horses approaching, I hunched my back and twisted my face. Reflected in the still water of the well was an older woman, her face deformed by suffering and ignorance, no trace of youth or beauty remained. A little flare of amusement, like the pilot flame of a lamp, flickered inside me. The soldiers would come, search the village for virgins, and finding none would depart in disgust, shouting ribald jokes about country girls. Like most young women with adoring parents, I had no idea that I was living a spoiled, sheltered existence.

The sound of horse hooves striking stone, coming closer, an ominous animal drum that echoed the beating of my heart. I bent further over the well, clutching my wooden bucket, waiting for them to pass. Six horses, no, seven, trotting nearly in unison, their riders magnificent in the Sultan's livery, Arabian mares dancing across the dull stones of my village courtyard. God, they were beautiful, it was like a sight from another world. Briefly, ever so briefly, I looked up, for I was a vil-lage girl and had never seen such a thing. And in that instant, I caught the eye of the lead rider, an older man with green eyes and blonde hair, and

found myself unable to move. It was only when his flame-coloured mare had trotted into the centre of the courtyard, her hooves striking sparks from the stones, that I was able to look away. It was too late. My parents had changed my clothes, dirtied my face, cut my hair and stained my teeth, but they could do nothing, nothing at all about my eyes. My eyes betrayed me.

Thinking of my beloved parents, I am too sad to tell you about my journey across the desert to the Sultan's palace, tied to the back of the chestnut mare. Isolated and alone, long days passed with the horsemen trotting in perfect formation around me, a four-legged cage. At night we would stop, only at night. I was so sore that I would lie on my back and watch the desert stars rise and fall through the night sky, the air so cold that plumes of vapour rose from the steaming horses. Some-times we travelled through the night, in country where the jackals and the leopards loved to hunt, making it too dangerous to pitch tents. I saw from the soldiers' behaviour that they feared their master more than death, and my heart grew cold inside me.

Fearing attack by the armed gangs that roam this land, or an inopportune deflowering by one of his own soldiers (for they tell me that the Sultan's appetite is such that there are few virgins left) I sleep in the tent of the blonde rider. Each night I lie there, listening to his breathing, feeling his eyes on me. Secretly I reach down and flick my little

finger along the soft groove of my sex, imagining his face plunging between my legs, tongue rasping away the sticky liquid his scent has generated, green eyes blazing as he glances up at my face. There is a tension between us, unspoken, but stronger than anything I have ever felt before. Age and the desert sand have scoured hard vertical lines into his tanned cheeks. In the morning, just before dawn, when he leaves the tent to urinate, I glimpse the hard outline of his manhood impaling the soft fabric of his underclothes.

The lack of sleep, the shock of losing my family, and hard days of constant riding all conspire to weaken me. One day, I know not when, I wake to find that fever has invaded my body during the night. My limbs are red and limp as flannel, a cloud of heat rises from my chest and back, and yellow liquid streams from my nose and mouth. My hearing and sight are both affected; the world becomes soft and spongy, shapes as indistinct as if they were underwater. My skin is paper dry and thin with sweat. When I cannot stand up, they decide not to tie me to the horse, fearing it will kill me. A decision is made: we will camp here until the fever passes. Somewhere in the maelstrom, I hear the blonde soldier ordering his men to stand guard, gather firewood, search for food and water, pitch tents.

Day passes night and day again like the whirling patterns of a spinning top. When the fever finally passes, it takes with it the last vestiges of child-hood. All my plump curves are gone, leaving in their place this pale thinness, a narrow face in which my dark eyes burn like cinders dropped on cotton cloth. I have no strength, or shame, and

lie naked on my bed. I am dimly aware that the green-eyed man has nursed me through the sickness; I remember his blonde head hanging over me as he bathed my body with cool water, the exquisite touch of his hands as he washed vomit from my cheeks. As I recover, his careful ministrations continue. Twice a day he comes to me with a steaming bowl of water smelling of some green herb. He begins by dipping a white cloth into the water, squeezing out the excess liquid, and then gently rubs my body, working his way down from head to foot. Then (for he is very strong) he gently flips me over and begins work on my back, letting little drips of water run down the groove of my backbone. Once, as the water slipped and escaped in a little rivulet between the crack in my behind, I shuddered.

Alarmed, he cried out, 'Are you cold?', clearly fearing that the Sultan's prize would sicken before delivery.

'No,' I answered, raising my hips and arching my back so he could wash between my legs.

Apricot Silk

A knock at the cell's door interrupts my reverie. The Sultan's manservant stands there looking sheepish. 'My master wishes for you to enjoy the garden,' he mumbles, dropping his gaze. I stare at the boy, who blushes so red that his bronze skin turns the colour of a potter's kiln, and innocently ask him which garden he means. I was brought to this room at night, the green-eyed solider unable to look at me as he murmured his farewell. Apart from the Sultan's quarters and my own cell, I have little knowledge of the palace and its surrounds. 'The marble courtyard with peacocks and lemon trees,' answers the boy, his country accent becoming stronger as he wistfully adds, 'it is very fine.'

I climb out of bed and stand there, stark naked, in front of the boy. 'You will help me dress,' I tell him, knowing that a lady's maid (the blonde woman with the unremarkable face) is waiting outside, but enjoying the consternation rippling across his face. Sensing that it would be fatal to contradict the Sultan's current plaything, he complies, coming towards me with a neat armful of clothes, laid out the previous evening by an unknown hand while I visited the Sultan in his quarters.

The boy's hands are shaking as he nervously shuffles in front of me, unsure of how to proceed. I pick up a pair of panties from the top of the pile, holding the tiny scrap of apricot silk delicately between thumb and forefinger. 'You will help me with these.' Little droplets of sweat stand out on the manservant's forehead and his face becomes even redder. He takes the underwear and kneels before me, stretching the gusset apart so I can dip first one toe and then the other into the leg holes. It is like testing the water at the bathing hole and, as if I am adjusting to cold water, I make no attempt to hurry. Having done so, I stand still waiting for him to continue; he takes a deep breath and slowly works the underwear upwards, over my calves, knees, past the curve of my thighs. When his face is level with my pubis, he inhales sharply, swallows, chokes, and launches into a coughing fit. I reach over and pat him on the back, my warm fur only inches away from his tongue. 'There, there,' I coo. He gathers his courage and in one swift move yanks the panties upward so they settle low on my hips.

I stretch upwards, glorying in my power, and the luck of having cheated death another night. I enjoy the sensation of having a young man pulling a slip over my head, button my gown, brush my hair, and finally coax my feet into jewelled slippers. I thank him and leave the room, looking forward to the feeling of the sun on my face. There have been too many days and nights spent in darkness.

Sky

Overhead the sky is a clear slice of blue heaven. Light bounces off the white marble, and I am blinded, pausing to sit under a lemon tree until my eyes adjust. At first all I can see is a kind of milky veil behind which shapes and objects shift and merge. Then, as my eyes adjust to the light, I see that I am sitting in an exquisite courtyard, with high rose-coloured stone walls, pale marble tiles and a fountain. I breathe deeply, smelling sweet jasmine, lemon, emerald-green plants and wet black earth. The tinkling sound of the fountain enters my body, bubbles and laughs its way around my bloodstream, washing away knots of tension in my spine, emerging from my mouth as a silvery laugh. I point my toes and watch a white peacock strut by. A thousand lemon blossom stars shine brightly against dark green foliage.

There is nobody in the courtyard. All is quiet, no windows overlook me, and for a time I enjoy the perfect pleasure of solitude. I sit and feel the sunlight quivering against my skin, the glory of warm stone under my legs. Birds sing overhead and the fountain chortles and flickers. After a little while though, the quietness begins to become oppressive, and inevitably my mind returns to the evening ahead. I feel cheated by last night's activities, and even vaguely angry. I'm not sure why. Musing on my anger, I stand and pace around the courtyard, searching for a solution to an impossible problem. And then, right in front of me, I see it: a small stack of books bound with a golden ribbon. I untie the ribbon and it falls open in a river of sparkling light. Taking the top book from the stack, I let the cover fall open where it will, and begin to read.

I breathe deeply, smelling sweet jasmine, lemon, emerald-green plants & wet black earth.

The Weight of Beauty

Once upon a time there was a beautiful princess who was loved by her mother and father, envied by her friends, and adored by many passionate suitors. She was so beautiful that even animals were struck dumb in her presence: cows would not moo, lambs couldn't bleat, and once the cock refused to crow, sending the whole village into a commotion when everyone slept late. Even the town's dogs, normally the happiest and least complex members of the animal kingdom, sat silent and love-struck in her presence. If the princess walked through the village, strangers would stop to thank her for her beauty, and the prettiest flowers would bitterly plunge their petalled heads underground. One spring morning, when the princess played in the palace garden, the magnolias were too jealous to blossom, songbirds sang dirges and the daffodils refused to open.

Of course, all this attention went to the princess' head. When she reached the age at which most young maidens are decently wed, she would spend long hours gazing in a mirror, slowly turning her flawless face this way and that. She would remain in front of the mirror all day and night, fascinated and aloof, as cold and still as a lump of ice. Her mother, worried that she may never have romping grandchildren to boast about, instructed her servants to keep the princess away from the mirror.

The princess' mother tried her best to organise an heir. When she invited a suitable prince to call upon their daughter, it was always difficult to get her into a room with him. She would often make charming excuses, 'I've got to wash my hair,' or would arrive, smile radiantly, and while the dazed prince was still searching for words, quickly make her escape. She avoided balls, refused to hunt, wouldn't consent to tea parties; in short, she circumvented all the social rituals so well designed to bring aristocratic young men and women into each other's orbit. Her ageing parents shook their heads and groaned.

'Where did we go wrong?' they asked each other.

One day, there was a great upheaval in their village. An exhausted messenger, riding a dusty black mare, galloped in from the desert, bringing word that Prince Caspian would soon visit. The local tavern owner quickly ushered the messenger into his establishment, for a drunk rider is known to communicate more efficaciously than a sober one, while someone else wiped the steaming horse down and let it sip from a jug of mint iced water. A crowd gathered at the tavern entrance, and slowly, as the messenger sat and ate roast lamb, drank cold ale, and bounced a fine serving wench on his lap, his story was relayed to those waiting outside.

Prince Caspian, said the messenger to the serving wench (who told the tavern owner, who whispered to the town's banker, who elbowed the writer and led him aside to murmur the news, who promptly proceeded to tell everyone) was a noble lord still fresh from battle with the barbarian tribes to the north. The messenger, who was keen to impress the wench, claimed that the Prince rode with the severed heads of his enemies bouncing along behind his horse like a string of children's toys. He was a nephew of the Sultan, in favour with the powerful Grand Vizier, rich, generous, kept a noble harem, was a good rider and handsome to boot. He was clearly an excellent match for any aspiring young lady.

When the princess' parents heard the news, they looked at each with glee. Although they were well-bred, they were not above waiting at tavern doors when the circumstances demanded (this was a very small town, not marked on any maps, so genuine news was rare). 'Wife!' exclaimed the husband, hugging her tight and dancing in a little circle like a jolly circus bear, 'This is the man for our girl! She cannot refuse such a mighty warrior.' And while the mother hugged her husband, and smiled into his face with seeming candour, in her heart she knew that such a match, though eminently desirable, was at most a distant chance.

'Husband,' she warned him gently, 'we must prepare our daughter.'

The next day, by a circuitous route, a note was sent to the messenger by the princess' parents. The note alluded to the princess' great beauty, noble birth, and matrimonial status. Having received this missive, relayed as it was by the hungover tavern owner – with a disappointed serving wench hovering in the background – the messenger could not decently refuse to pass it on to his master. Wearily, he saddled his black mare, kissed the serving wench one last time, and galloped off into the desert to find Prince Caspian. As he rode, he mentally reviewed the town gossip, as told by the

serving wench: a fine woman! With his horse's hooves pounding into the desert sand, and his hangover worsening with each jolt, he tried to distract himself with the intriguing tale of the vain princess and her addictive mirror.

The villagers watched him go. They stood there, waiting until the dust raised by his mare was nothing more than a memory, and the straight line of the horizon was unblemished by any movement, for a desert swallows life like a hungry catfish takes a hook. Then people turned to each other, some disappointed, some hopeful, either proclaiming, 'The Prince will come!' or crying with equal confidence, 'The Prince will not come!' For it was well-known that a handsome prince, possessing wealth and a noble harem, sometimes failed to see the need for a wife, or legitimate offspring, much to the inevitable chagrin of his royal mother.

Back at the princess' palace, the mother rushed upstairs to her daughter's bedroom, for she was an optimist and felt sure that the prince would return. She discovered the girl sitting entranced in front of her mirror, turning her shining hair through long cool fingers. And suddenly, for no reason, the mother thought of the princess' birth, all those years ago. She had been a breech baby, and the memory of all that pain and blood, and the thought of a noble prince rapidly galloping off into the desert, caused something to spark deep inside her. A wall of feeling hit her in the chest like a ship's prow. 'Will you stop looking in that fucking mirror!' she screamed, voice raw as a fishwife. She grabbed her daughter's shoulder, meaning to shake some sense into her; at the same moment, the princess seized the mirror frame to steady herself, and so the whole thing came crashing to the

ground. Jagged pieces of reflective glass were strewn across the floor, showing a thousand fragmented family portraits: a shocked princess, face pale with fright; her mother, anger replaced by sorrow, gently touching her shoulder. And the young princess sobbed for the mirror had been her most treasured possession.

Days passed, the prince did not come, and the princess was inconsolable. She gathered the broken shards of glass into a jar and sat holding it up to the light so that it sparkled like a starburst. She wandered aimlessly, peering into muddy puddles, standing by the waterhole, entreating the cook to polish her copper pans more perfectly, breathing onto silver spoons and rubbing them with her own gown, twisting and turning in front of windows. She was observed frantically rubbing an old metal tray in a futile attempt to make it shine. At last, her parents – in desperation – promised that they would visit the town's only market to see if another mirror could be procured. The next morning, they all rose early, the princess now happy and fresh as a bird, her cheeks the soft pink of spring roses, her sunset-coloured gown embroidered with flowers and brilliantly coloured finches. That morning, as they walked through the village, even the sun refused to shine, so ashamed was he by her unearthly radiance.

Into town they went, searching the market for a mirror, wandering from stall to stall. Her normally upright parents stooped to engage in avid conversation any unshaven desert trader, any dishevelled antiques dealer. But there were no mirrors to be found. In a small town, in the middle of a vast desert, a place not marked on any maps, a mirror is considered an eccentric luxury. At last, when they were just about to give up and go home, they happened upon a dusty tent, right on the edge of

the market, with a stranger sitting out front. The princess' father stepped forward, his old voice breaking with sorrow, and asked the man if he happened to have any mirrors to sell.

'As a matter of fact,' replied the stranger, 'I have six.'

'Six!' exclaimed the father, turning to his wife and daughter, honest face full of beaming pleasure, 'when we only needed one.' He turned to ask the stranger for the price. But the man looked at him oddly and replied, 'We will discuss that later.' He gestured for the princess to enter the tent. Before her parents could stop her, the young woman leapt forward like a fawn, desperate for her first glimpse of a reflective surface in over a week.

Inside sat Prince Caspian, legs crossed, arms resting on his knees, perfectly at home with a huge mastiff lying at his feet. When the princess entered the tent, the mastiff raised his wrinkled head to sniff the air, beat his tail a few times, and then went back to sleep. 'Welcome,' said Prince Caspian, mockingly sweeping his hand around the interior of the small tent, a gesture that took in the dirt floor and the dusty canvas walls, and gave the princess a little bow of his head. But she was in a hurry, and did not acknowledge him, so keen was she to behold her own beauty.

'Where are the mirrors?' she interrupted him, looking quickly around, 'The man outside said you had six.' Prince Caspian smiled and stretched in his chair, a movement that caused the mastiff to grunt and fart. The smell of rotting eggs drifted upwards, penetrating the musty air of the tent.

'He is old and blind,' explained the prince, 'but I love this dog like a brother, he has been with me many years.' Then he bounded to his feet, took the princess by her hand, and led her to some bundles of black cloth lying near the back of the tent. 'There they are,' he said, pointing sardonically at the waiting bundles, and stood back to watch her reaction.

In a flurry of impatience, the princess surged forward, ripping the fabric from the bundles. She grabbed the first mirror, quickly raised it to head height, and nearly dropped it with a gasp of horrified astonishment. Turning to the next mirror, she lifted it to her face, and again a harsh cry escaped her lips. Four more times she seized a mirror, only to behold her reflection and cry out in passionate disgust. Angrily she turned to the prince, speechless with indignation and shock. 'They are from a travelling circus, an old desert trader sold them to me,' drawled the prince in his laconic way. 'I brought them because they entertained me, and because,' he added, scrutinising the beautiful girl, 'one never knows when such things may come in handy. One makes you look tall and thin, another short and fat, two more twist your face into a monkey grimace, and the remaining pair... well, it's certainly unexpected, I'm not quite sure how they do it.' Not believing her eyes, the princess again grabbed the last mirror; once more she saw her lovely face reflected with pointed jackal ears.

Seeing herself as short, fat, and disfigured was tremendously unsettling for the young woman. Sensing, for the first time, the unbelievable truth that one day she too would grow old, she burst into tears. Crying piteously, she howled at the shortness of time, the quick passing of youth. Roused by the sound of sobs, the slumbering mastiff awoke and staggered to his rheumatoid old feet. Trailing a thin stream of bright yellow urine as he crossed the floor, the dog raised his stinking muzzle to nuzzle the princess. Despite her

vanity, the princess was a kind girl, and recognising the dog's good-hearted attempt to comfort her, she gently stroked his ears with her lily-white hand. Seeing her caress his dog's fetid head caused a small explosion in the prince's heart: he fell madly in love with her, and more importantly, never changed his mind. And maybe it was the circus mirrors, or perhaps it was being alone in a small tent with a handsome man, or even the approval of an old, blind dog, but when the princess emerged from the tent her cheeks were uncharacteristically flushed, her hair was dishevelled, and her eyes shone like young stars.

Suck

A touch on my arm startles me. I had been so engrossed in my book that I had not noticed the sun dip behind the palace roof, the tree's shadow grow long and ragged, and the sounds of the night birds slowly build. A nightingale's song drifts down from somewhere high above. Standing in front of me is the young manservant, his eyes downcast, seemingly recovered from his flustered condition, though I notice some promising red blotches staining the pure skin of his neck. 'It is time,' he says simply. 'My master wants you.'

I rise, placing the book back on the pile, and stretch my back. Like the princess of the tale, I have been sitting still for so long that my muscles have cramped. A surge of panic suddenly overtakes me: I have not prepared a story for his evening entertainment. Then fear is replaced by a kind of brooding, burning, angry lust as I wonder whether the Sultan had left the story of the princess as a message. I recall his mock condescension of the previous evening, the ironic bow as he handed me a towel. Surely not, I tell myself, I opened the book at random; he couldn't have known where I would start reading. And besides, I am nothing like that girl!

Servants lead me to his quarters where I find him staring out the window at the gathering dark, his broad shoulders forming a triangular silhouette; I adore the heart-shaped musculature of his strong torso. Again, anger and lust well up in me; so he

thinks I'm spoiled, does he? I stalk over to the tall wardrobe full of costumes and bad-temperedly flick through them until I find a large dress. The Sultan turns to face me, a small smile playing on his curved lips. I throw the dress down at his feet and pout. 'Put it on,' I command, trying to sound tough and brave, but actually just like a coddled brat.

The Sultan's grin increases a fraction, and he moves towards me with his lion's grace, dark eyes full of secret amusement. As always, when he gets close, I notice the way the hair curls across his broad chest, and his scent: a deep pungent odour, somewhere between smoke, blood and spice. I sniff the air greedily. 'Put it on!' I squeal, pointing to the piece of red silk lying on the floor. He gives me a mocking curtsy, picks up the dress with disdain, and drags it over his head, clumsy and fast, completely different to how a woman would do it. For some reason, the sight makes me wet. I reach forward and adjust the sleeves and long skirt of the gown, smoothing the shining fabric so it curves as it should, letting my hands linger on the hard body beneath the silk. He stands there, utterly comfortable, waiting to see what I will do. Once again, I am reminded of a cat, choosing when and how it will dispose of a rodent, but deciding to have a little fun first. My anger returns like a white-hot sheet of liquid metal.

I punch my fists into his shoulders, shoving him back across the room, until he slams up against the wall. For a moment I see alarm in his eyes, then that terrible, complacent calm, the endless confidence of the powerful. I twist my hands into his hair and wrench his head back, biting his neck so hard that I draw blood, kicking his legs apart so he is spreadeagled against the wall. I reach down into the neck of the gown and cruelly pinch his nipples, spit on my fingers and rub them against his penis, then embed my long nails into his thighs. His mouth is closed so I lick it open with my long tongue, forcing it into the back of his mouth, tasting every inch of the wet cavern. My hands force the skin of his foreskin back and forwards, sharp thrusts with a tight grip, until his face his red and his cock slippery with sweat. I bite his neck hard, slap him across the face, scoring his buttocks into thin red welts with my clawed hands.

And then I relent. I gently lift his dress so that the silk brushes his swollen organ and he moans with ecstasy. I drop to my knees, cooing entreaties, calling him my beloved, my warrior, my lover, as I lick, lick, lick. First delicate little butterfly kisses on the tip; then long, slow strokes with my tongue up and down the shaft, luxuriating in the feeling of mouth on velvet-smooth skin. I lick and kiss my way down the groove where his powerful thighs meet his muscular abdomen, nuzzle the wiry hair of his sex, spit on my palm and let it rotate around the end of his cock. The veins are pulsing and the skin has flushed to a ripe purple when I slide the whole length into my mouth, sucking with a steady rhythmic pressure, letting my lips caress the tip as I go back for another stroke. He moans, writhes against the wall, ridiculous and glorious in his red silk. I tease him, twisting my hair around his sex, brushing the sides of my face against his shaft

and then quickly turning to again consume its whole length in my hot wet mouth.

When I think he is about to climax, I rub his juice and my saliva between my breasts and insert his penis into the crevice. He bucks against the wall like an unbroken colt, I push the tip into my erect nipple and unable to wait any longer he comes, jetting semen across my face and chest. I rub the viscous liquid into my hair, cradle his spent penis between my breasts, lightly stroke the sensitive area behind his testicles. Spasms judder through his body, squeezing a few more drops onto my waiting breasts; as he arches forward, I hear his hoarse breathing and feel sweat drop onto my back. His hands, which have gripped my shoulders like a vice, relax and affectionately stroke my hair, teasing it into strands and letting it fall. With the part of my mind that is always cold, I realise that I have survived another night, perhaps even two.

Seed

That night, after I leave the Sultan's quarters, sticky with semen and sweat, I have the most peculiar dream. I dream that I am lying out under a gigantic full moon, the silver light as bright as sunshine, the odd pull of lunar power animating my blood in peculiar new ways. I lie naked on dark earth, black dirt that stinks of animal manure and old rocks, cool dampness caressing my hot skin. Somehow, I can hear the trees growing, the sound of a distant jackal's heartbeat, the noise of plants stirring underground. I am surrounded by the rustling noises of things growing, flourishing, feeding, and dying. As the moon pulses overhead, I notice small green shoots of new plants bursting from my skin, rising upwards in delicate hair-like strands, yearning for the moonlight. I watch buds form and burst open to reveal silver flowers, orchids, their throats speckled with tiny dark scarlet dots, a magenta tongue hanging from their lips. I remember picking a flower that springs from my chest and beholding it with fascination.

I wake with my tongue cloven to the roof of my mouth and my breasts smelling of his pleasure. I ponder the strange feeling of power and transgression as I knelt before him and raised his dress. An old soldier once told me about the trials of war, where men feed with the hunger of starving beasts. He said that sometimes you only know you've crossed a boundary when you look back and see it behind you. If only, I think, I could learn to live like this in the daylight. I drift back to sleep.

I am surrounded by the rustling noises of things growing, flourishing, feeding, & dying.

The Tempest

Many years ago, there was a small cottage on the side of a steep mountain in a fir tree lined valley. The wind poured down from the top of the mountain in a freezing torrent of blue air, shooting through the narrow valley, and emerging on the other side in a purple cloud of sharp pine needles. Although pine trees usually grow straight and true, the trees in this particular valley were on such a lean that if the wind had ever shifted direction, they would have all fallen over like last summer's dry grass.

In the cottage lived an elderly couple who longed for a child. They were both fit and strong, with olive skin and lively brown eyes, and could not understand why the gods had denied them their only desire. The old woman spent many years decorating a child's room, and her husband turned wooden toys and painted the walls a cheerful yellow, yet the years had passed and no baby arrived. Soon all the little toys and the beautifully carved cot accumulated a thick blanket of dust, and the couple never visited the room, preferring to keep the door closed and their hearts intact.

One night, at the very end of winter, the old man noticed an odd green light at the top of the mountain. 'Wife,' he said, gesturing towards the very highest peak, 'I believe we are in for some foul weather.' The very moment the words left his mouth, the strongest wind either of them had ever seen rushed through the valley, bringing with it a flurry of icy stones and frozen leaves. 'Husband,' said the woman, 'this is going to be a very bad night indeed.' Quickly they brought their chickens into the living room, led the cow into the kitchen, nestled the sheep and their newborn lambs in the bedroom. The wife stoked the fire, and the husband brought his shovel inside, knowing that in the morning they would have to dig their way out through deep snow.

But it didn't snow that night, nor the next night or the one after. Instead, the wind howled like a rabid dog, hurling branches and pieces of mountain boulder against the cottage walls. Once, it seemed to the woman, as she stood by the kitchen sink, that she saw a spotted deer blown past the window. And the man could have sworn he saw a shaggy brown bear tumbling head over heels through the sky. The tempest never stopped, but seemed to get louder and stronger, until by the third night the man and his wife wrapped woollen scarves around their heads to keep out both the cold and the noise. And then, quite suddenly, the wind stopped.

The old man and woman looked at one another with relief. Tap-tap-tap. In the eerie silence, something was tapping at their door. It knocked three times, then paused, and knocked again. Tap-tap-tap. They looked at each other with dread, then the old woman took a step towards the door, and her husband took two, and she took three, and finally they found themselves standing at the doorway, each with one hand on the doorknob and the other clasping their spouse. Tap-tap-tap. The cottage was in an isolated spot, far from any village, and the old couple never visited their neighbours, as the sight of all those romping babies was too painful to bare. And if it was not a person at the door, then what manner of creature could survive such a tempest?

With a mighty heave, the man and woman threw open the cottage door. They looked around, puzzled, as there was nothing of interest outside except for a great deal of smashed timber and piles of pounded leaves. Then they heard an odd squeak and looking down saw a small bundle of grey blankets placed neatly on the dirt, and peering out through a gap in the cloth, a cheerful infant with enormous black eyes. The man looked at the woman, and the woman looked at the man, and they said to one another, 'The gods have answered our prayers!' They picked the baby up, took it inside by the fire, quickly warmed the child's bedroom and swept away the dust. By dusk that evening, they were looking down at a sleeping infant in her hand-carved cot, tucked beneath delicately-knitted blankets, soft as duckling feathers. And the old couple's faces glowed with warmth and contentment.

Years passed and the child grew like the proverbial weed. First, she was a chubby little baby, then an energetic toddler, a skinny child of ten, and eventually a young woman. She was a tall person with thick dark hair covering most of her body, a sharp profile, and eyes like the night sky. Her adoring parents loved her like the sun at midnight. They never uncovered the story of her mysterious delivery, and had long since stopped talking about it, preferring to keep their hearts intact. Sometimes, late at night, the wife would cling to her husband and whisper, 'What if the thing that brought her to us decides to take her back?' And sometimes the husband would say to the wife, 'Why have we been given this great gift but asked for nothing in return?' On

such nights, the elderly couple would brew themselves nettle tea and honey, sit by the fire holding hands, and pray silently to any god they could remember.

One evening, when the girl was away visiting friends in the village, the husband and wife sat on the porch watching the sun set through the pine trees. They felt a slight tremor beneath their rocking chairs. It was a dull vibration that buzzed for a few seconds and then stopped. 'Must be a rock fall on the mountain side,' said the man to his wife. Then they felt it again: a deep vibration that tingled the very core of their bones. The wife swallowed. 'Falling rocks have probably set off an avalanche,' she said. And then the sound came again, reverberating through their bodies and shaking the cottage to its foundations. 'I have no idea what that is,' admitted the husband, as his wife looked at him with desperate appeal.

Deep in the pine forest, they could see something moving. Whatever it was, the thing was large, shook the ground like thunder as it walked, and was heading straight towards the cottage. The husband made to dash into the house, to grab some weapon or another, but the old woman seized his hand. 'Whatever it is,' she said, 'an axe or blade will not stop it.' They stood there together, waiting for the huge form to emerge from the darkness, watching as sturdy pine trees shook like bunches of feathers. Finally, a monstrous being stepped out from the trees and stood before them.

It was an enormous fir tree, the oldest and the largest either of them had ever seen. The bark was knotted deep in rivulets of rough fur, with arm-like branches spreading far across the darkening sky. Thousands of pine needles covered its body and waved in the cool air like spiky fur. The tree walked towards them, stopped a short distance from the rocking chairs, and although the old couple could not see any eyes, they felt sure the creature was watching them. Its gaze seemed to take in their cottage, built so carefully from rough-skinned logs; their carved rocking chairs; the little chicken coop and animal enclosures surrounded by neat paling fences; an axe propped up by the cottage door; and a blue-grey corkscrew of smoke emerging from the stone chimney.

A stillness, then, and the first stirrings of a light breeze that drifted down from the mountain top like the gentlest of snows. Just a slight zephyr at first, then a wave of cold wind that grew and grew, raging and foaming in an invisible torrent, shaking the trees like twigs, bringing with it a rain of stinging pine needles and bitter dust. And a sound like a million dogs howling all at once. And a wind that hit the old man and woman like an iron hammer. And a dancing green light that lit up the sky like fire from another world. All at once it stopped.

The couple reached for each other's hands, feeling a sudden stiffness in their bodies, a deep reluctance overcome both bone and muscle. They stood there, fingers intertwined, feeling their blood slow to a wandering crawl, to their eyes harden and stop blinking, to the cooling of their skin and the last thuds of their human hearts. Although they could not bend their heads to look, they could feel the soles of their feet growing roots, long tendrils that burrowed blindly into the soil. Their clothing shrunk tight to their bodies, sticking to the skin in tight brown ridges and folds. And their spines, bent by age and work, reached up towards the sky in lines that were straight and true. By the time night fell, two fully grown fir trees stood in front of the cottage, their root systems lovingly intertwined.

In the pink mist of the following dawn, the little cottage continued its marvellous transformation. The rocking chairs sprouted fresh green leaves and busily sent roots

They stood there, fingers intertwined, feeling their blood slow to a wandering crawl, to their eyes harden & stop blinking, to the cooling of their skin & the last thuds of their human hearts.

down into the rich, dark soil. The rough-hewn logs of the cottage walls shot forth new boughs in every direction. The paling fence around the animal enclosures collapsed in a tangled mess of white blossom, and the freed animals rooted happily around on the forest floor. Even the axe by the door flourished, quickly growing into a dark red bush with brilliant yellow flowers.

By the time the girl returned from the village – laughing as she bid her friends goodbye and promising to visit them again soon – all that remained of the cottage was a grove of small trees, peaceful beasts, and flowering bushes. And towering above, two old fir trees watching over them all like kindly guardians.

Beast

Early the next morning, I open my eyes to find the manservant silently bustling around the room, laying out a pile of clothing, pouring water from a silver jug into a bowl for washing. I watch him for a while, feeling tired but unable to return to slumber. Idly I let my eyes trace the outline of his buttocks as he bends over, arranging things, quietly wiping surfaces, leaving the room only to return with a large plate of fresh fruit. He leaves a second time, this time returning with a bowl of fresh figs, honey and sticky yoghurt.

My stomach begins to rumble, and I quickly sit up. Startled, the manservant immediately lowers his eyes and adopts a deferential pose, so different from the efficient busyness of the moment before. 'Good morning,' he murmurs. 'My master wishes you slept well. He orders that after breakfast, you are to be shown the living treasures of the palace menagerie.' I incline my head in thanks. It is the longest speech the servant has ever made, which makes me curious: does he know something I do not?

Taking my seat, I quickly dispatch a plate of plump figs, stuffed with soft cheese and chopped walnuts, drizzled with honey and adorned with a creamy mountain of yoghurt. I am impatient to see the animals, and I order the servants to dress me quickly, stuffing my feet into the shoes so quickly that I almost slip and fall. A nightly encounter with my own mortality has stripped away any pretence of breeding, dignity, or grace that I once possessed. I bound down the stairs,

two at a time, the servants strung out behind, panting in an untidy gaggle. I am forced, however, to stop at the bottom of the staircase, halted by a heavy wooden door with an iron lock. There I wait while the manservant fumbles and jiggles his bunch of keys, searching for the correct one, eventually sliding it into the hole and turning it with a loud click.

Outside. I turn my face to glory in the sun, a flower that has lived in darkness for too long. I feel my eyes drinking in the light and warmth, my body starts to relax, the eternal anxiety begins to dissipate. Stretching my fingers tight, I shake them lightly, imagining tension flying out of the ends like some kind of polluted spirit. I roll my shoulders and greedily snuff up the ordinary smells of dirt, light, rock and sand.

'Where are the animals?' I demand, gazing around me.

The manservant looks sheepish as he replies, 'You must wear a blindfold.'

So, I think, the Sultan trusts me, but not that much, still afraid that his pretty bird will remember the layout of his palace and flee one dark night. If only it were so. They slip a heavy cloth blindfold over my eyes and the manservant gently takes my arm. We shuffle forward, my hearing intensified by the loss of sight, steps made timid by the unknown terrain. We walk a long way, down another flight of stairs, through one, no, two sets of doors and past an iron gate that creaks and

40

protests as rusted hinges screech open. I feel the air change. We are near trees, there is the smell of things growing, green hay and the pungent stench of animal dung. I step in a pool of liquid, which splashes up in a waft of yellow urine. Then they slip the blindfold from my face.

All around me are cages. And overhead are trees, full of fruit, their boughs heavy with a thousand parrots. In the cages I see a leopard, monkey, lion, tiger, even a kangaroo. At a distance, a servant is proudly leading a gigantic grey animal with two long bone poles protruding from its head; later they tell me that this is an elephant, the only one in the kingdom. Another servant staggers past wheeling a barrow full of severed human limbs. I watch as he hurls a leg to the shiny black jaguar, pokes an arm through the bars at a lion, gingerly offers a hand to the tiger. The manservant, hovering beside me, keen to report the menagerie visit as a success, coughs and mutters something that sounds like, 'From the hospital.' I watch a leopard snapping at a pelvis and turn away, sickened.

They usher me to the aviary, and it is something so splendid that, artist though I am, I feel words begin to fail me. Overhead it rises into the sky, so high that I am sure that on a misty morning, clouds will gather beneath its roof. We enter through a meshed door, stand in a small antechamber, while another servant unlocks a second door. When I enter the aviary, I am reminded of the presence of God; the distant roof is the bell tower of the world. Birds of a thousand colours dart past like flying jewels. And there are butterflies too, vast as plates, flittering past on blue wings, as large as the smaller birds. We walk into the centre of the space, under the vast dome of the roof, and find ourselves in a clearing, a narrow circle where it is possible to see the sky. It is damp at the base of the trees, a rainforest where frogs croak from inside mossy logs, and a small creek tinkles and then disappears into the scrub. I wander through the trees, powdery butterfly wings caressing my face, drawn by the sound of water. As it becomes clearer, I push aside thick jungle vines, my feet scrunching on round pebbles, as I glimpse long-legged waders hurrying away into the underbrush.

A stream, the rarest thing in a desert, is babbling and dancing its silver brown way across the jungle floor. Beside the water is a large smooth rock and I lean against it, finding it comfortably warm against my back, feeling myself grow sleepy.

'This,' says the manservant quietly, 'is where my master comes to think.'

I climb onto the rock's back, curved as a cow spine, speckled with sunlight from the faraway sky. 'Leave me now,' I tell him, 'I shall sleep for a while.'

He walks backwards out of the clearing, but I know he will not go far: they cannot risk losing me. I listen to the water tinkling past, singing its way around the foot of my rock, sounds of birds calling to each other far above, the chirp-chirp-chirp of frog song, a million small clicks and scratches of things growing. For the first time since I left my parents' house, I sleep like an innocent child.

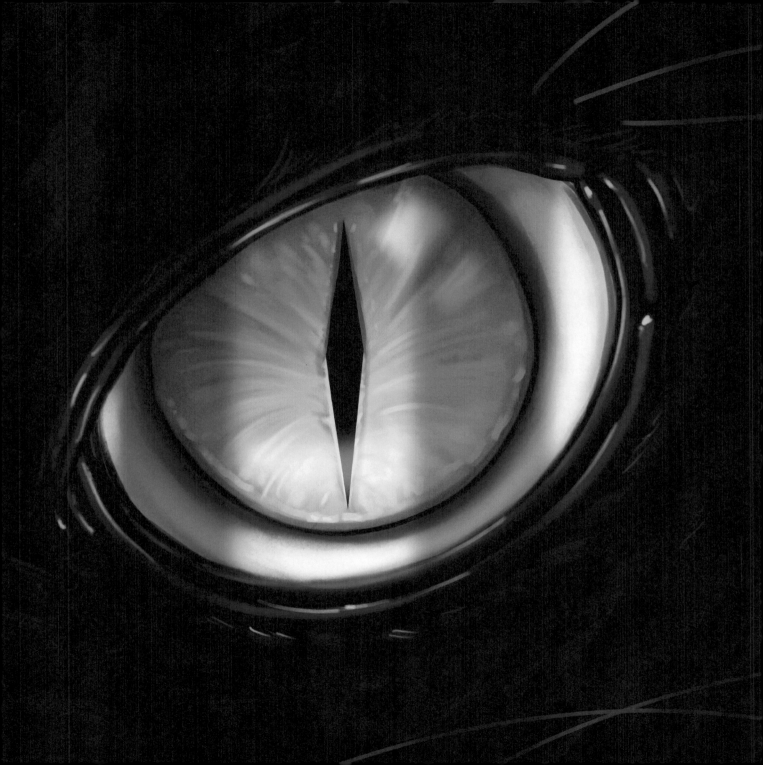

The Hummingbird's Song

It is not clear to me whether I am awake or asleep when the hummingbird comes. Perching on the end of my rock, the bird peers into my face and I realise with a little shock that its eyes are blue, human blue, and full of all the emotion and empathy of a person's face.

'Are you awake?' it asks me, leaning forward to poke my upper arm with its scimitar beak.

'That depends,' I reply, 'whether there is such a thing as a talking bird.'

'Of course, there isn't,' the hummingbird snaps crossly. 'How foolish of you to think such a thing.' It bad-temperedly pushes a few feathers into place, preens an already immaculate wing, stamping its red-banded legs for good measure.

I sit up and the bird levitates until it is hovering level with my head. The bright eyes gaze intently into mine, the heartbeat-fast beating of its wings fan my face.

'Forgive me,' I tell the bird, allowing the dream to have its own life. 'I don't know what made me think such a thing.' The hummingbird smiles, beak stretching into a good-natured grin; I sense that humour is the creature's default position. It lands lightly on my head, twists grey claws into my skull and politely asks,

'Are you ready now?'

'Quite ready,' I respond, though for what I am unsure.

In one heartbeat I am sitting on a large, warm rock with a hummingbird attached to my skull. In the next, I am airborne. The little bird bears me aloft with fragile wings, my body trailing behind as light as feather down. We rise upwards through a mist of butterflies, push through dense foliage, and emerge on top of the tree canopy, in direct sunlight, a wide sapphire sky arching far above. It is the highest I have ever been. I see this land as I have never seen it before: vast deserts, distant mountains, a great river that winds like a silver snake across the plains, veins of roads stretching across the scorched skin of the country. I am suffused with wonder. But then I notice that my companion is becoming impatient, leaning forward to peer anxiously into my face, claws still clasped to bone.

'I didn't bring you up here to admire the view,' says the bird in a tart voice. 'Lots of things are beautiful, it really means very little.' Seeing my incomprehension, the frustrated hummingbird digs its claws further into my skull. The pain snaps me out of my dazed reverie. 'Don't you see,' cries the bird, suddenly looking at me with my mother's eyes, so patient and kind, 'you've forgotten who you are?' We rise higher until the sun burns down on my head and I can see the whole of the giant river, its sides dotted with cities and villages, the ebb and the flow of the landscape. 'It's a big world out there,' whispers the little bird into my ear. And with these words still ringing in my head, I wake to find the manservant waiting patiently by my side, his presence as inevitable as the night.

Harness

By the time we return to the palace, it is late afternoon and already the sun is beginning to send long shadows creeping up the stone walls of my room, dappling the floor with spots of light. Feeling dazed by my brief sleep on the rock, and the splendours of the aviary, I lean against the windowsill and consider the evening's entertainment. From my window, I can see a small section of the street. On this particular afternoon, I watch a donkey pulling a wooden cart laden with bags of seed, a long thin whip caressing its fly-blown haunches. A complex series of straps holds the leather bridle and harness in place. Inspired, I grab pencil and paper, make a quick drawing, then call for the blonde maid and ask her to bring me the palace carpenter.

A complex series of straps holds the leather bridle & harness in place.

He arrives quickly, an old man clutching a bag of tools. His hands are rough with work and his face is deeply lined by the sun. A good man: humble and uncomplicated, working hard, keeping his head down, patiently serving his master. In my village there were many such men and women, and although I respected them, we had nothing in common. There was always this sense that although we were using the same words, we spoke a different language, with a gulf in meaning too vast to be crossed; this both sorrowed and exalted me.

I hand him the drawing, explaining that he has only until sundown to build my design. He gazes at me with worried incomprehension, fingering the drawing as if it were a legal document, so I lean closer and whisper what the contraption does. I look at the old man's hairy shell of an ear, as my words tumble over each other; I sense his embarrassment as his face goes pale. When I finish, he bows and almost runs from the room, nearly hitting the doorframe in his haste.

Night

Later that evening, I order the servants to keep the Sultan out of his bedchamber while the carpenter does his work. Intrigued by the sound of hammers, he paces the hallway outside the room, restlessly smoking a cigarette, impatient with lust. I glimpse him striding up and down the stone corridors, his shadow ghostly in the candlelight, a dark cloak billowing out behind him. He has been away all day, riding far to settle some bloody business, and is still wearing his leather riding boots. I am reminded of bats, creatures of the night, or certain birds of prey, with their lethal eyes concealed under rawhide hoods.

We make our preparations, candles are lit, and then I send the servants away. They leave in a hushed silence. The carpenter's young mate sneaks a final backwards glance, until the carpenter pushes him roughly through the door. When the Sultan is finally allowed to enter his bedchamber, he finds me suspended in space. A complex arrangement of leather straps, chains and buckles fasten around my slim body. I am horizontal to the floor, facing the ground, naked, immobile, suspended at groin height, my arms and legs outstretched like a flying fox, head encased in a tight-fitting leather helmet that leaves only my face free. A chain runs from a collar at my neck and loops down to connect at a silver fastening near my groin; another chain is strapped tight across my breasts, metal biting into the flesh. Beneath me, on a dark cloth, lie the items I have so carefully selected: a thin horse whip, the leather blade soft as butter but capable of a terrific sting (I have already tested it); a silver bowl of warm oil; a carved malachite dildo, the green stone smooth, icy, and flawless.

The Sultan circles me, viewing the contraption from all angles, choosing his pleasure. I enjoy the click of his boot heels striking the marble floor, ricocheting through the silence, and feel myself grow slippery with longing. Although I cannot see him, I can feel him become hard, sense the change in the room, the sudden sweet pulse of desire smoking from his body like a gas. I smell burning incense and candle wax, warm horse scent still clinging to his boots, freshly pierced leather, and the indefinable pungency of an aroused male. Lulled by the sight of candlelight flickering on the walls, I am surprised when he drops down onto his knees and thrusts his tongue into my vagina, caressing it with deep, slow strokes. Almost immediately he stops, circles me again, takes up a position at my head, and unexpectedly bends to grace my mouth with his tongue. We kiss, his wet tongue searching and receiving, a mutual flow of energy that transcends the bondage I have assumed. I sense all his gratitude in that kiss.

Then he is off again, walking around me, I hear the sound of clothing being unbuttoned and then his penis is rubbing against the lips of my cunt, teasing a little, pushing in a fraction so that just the head is encased in my wetness, then withdrawing and leaving me gasping for more. For some reason, though we have experienced every conceivable sexual act together, the Sultan prefers not to penetrate me with his cock. And how I have ached for it! Now he simply plays at the entrance, slipping his finger into the crease of the vulva, as if removing the stone from a ripe apricot, and fucking me with his prehensile tongue. When I am wet, my cunt slimy with juice, skin red as beetroot, he again breaks off to resume his slow pacing.

He gives the contraption a little push and, pleased with the way the arrangement of pulleys and blocks makes me swing, pushes a little harder. Bracing himself, he holds my hips in a firm grip and bounces me backwards and forwards against the rock-hard flesh of his sex, enjoying the power, refusing to give me what I want, while he lets me swing a little more. Soon I am gasping with excitement. I hear the whispering sound of the whip flying through the air and then the bee sting pain of it connecting with my buttocks, I beg him for more and he obliges, landing six hard strokes deep into the velvety flesh. I know that in the morning they will be wide red stripes. Then he drops, squirms underneath me, lying on the floor looking up at me, a surprisingly warm smile animating his cruel mouth. Tickling my nipples with the tip of the whip, he lies masturbating on the marble floor, his beautiful member pointing towards my groin, out of reach and untouchable, the tip glistening with my juice.

Standing again, he comes around to my head, inserts his cock into my mouth and I suck, holding onto him with all my might, my lips compressed tight around his shaft. He laughs as he breaks free, the suction so strong that its release sounds like a loud fart, and picks up the malachite dildo. This time when he stands behind me, he inserts the whole smooth length of the thing, the coldness of the stone against hot flesh driving me into a frenzy, my body bucking and writhing so that the chains jingle and the leather straps creak and cut into my flesh. When my orgasm comes, I call his name, his real name, over and over again. I sob out my love, my love, frantically try and tear free of the straps so I can reach him, pouring out my tangled web of feelings in a great confused stream. He unbuckles the straps, and I fall to the floor. He holds me, our arms wrapped around each other, bodies wet with sweat. At that moment, I am unable to tell where his body ends and mine begins: somehow, we have fused and become one.

The Tiger Bride

That night, unaccustomed to the strange sensation of sleeping in the Sultan's bed, I wake while it is still dark. I cannot say what roused me: maybe it was the sound of a nightingale calling outside the chamber window, or perhaps it was the quiet noise that a man makes when he wants to unobtrusively leave a bed. Either way, I wake up, skin salty with sweat, to find myself in an empty bed. Like all women who discover themselves abandoned in this manner, I am both resentful and quietly relieved.

I call out to the manservant, and ever vigilant he ghosts out of the darkness, pausing to hover at my bedside. 'Tell me a story,' I demand, then seeing the black shadows under his eyes – for he guards me for his master like a tireless dog – add, 'Please.' His eyebrows, which have set in a vee-shaped scowl (though discreetly hidden) retract and he settles comfortably by my side. Picking up a book from the bedside table, and opening it to a well-worn crease, he says, 'This is a story about a beast who lost his daughter at a game of cards.'

Once upon a time, in a faraway land, further than the world's end, where the green waterfalls tip off the edge of the earth, and fall through limitless white clouds, there lived an old man. The old man's wife had died young, leaving behind a clever daughter to be cared for by an elderly nurse. The nurse taught the young girl embroidery and other fine needlework and loved her like a mother. She told her that there was enormous potency in such handicrafts, and that sewing was like casting a spell. She promised the young girl that if she sewed patiently enough, one day her hands would work powerful magic.

Years passed quick-slow, as they do when children are around, and the girl grew into a glorious young woman. She was a dutiful daughter, who obeyed her father, but she was no fool, and knew that as a parent he was not all that he should be. She watched helplessly as the old man's monthly card games gradually became weekly events, then rapidly turned into daily encounters, and finally dominated every hour of his waking life. She watched him drink when he lost, and drink when he won, and slowly their house fell apart, and her clothing became thinner. But there was no money to fix either, even though there was a seemingly inexhaustible supply for his games, so she patched her dresses and bravely tried to ignore the rain coming in through the roof.

One night a dreadful storm howled across their country, bringing with it a night so bad that rain flew in through the holes in the roof like ocean waves, and even the old man looked up anxiously, temporarily distracted from his cup. A great crash of thunder shook the house, and when the noise faded it was replaced by another noise, somewhat quieter but much closer: a sinister rap-rap-rap. On this accursed night, a night when only a madman would travel, outside in the hail and the lightning, someone or something was knocking at their door.

The girl crept to the top of the stairs, and remaining hidden, for she was wearing her oldest nightgown, peered down into the dark antechamber. From her hiding place she saw her father hobble towards the entrance and swing open the heavy timber door, which creaked loudly, revealing a tall figure standing outside. She could not see his face because he was wearing a hooded cloak, only the tip of his boots, which were of the blackest leather and soaked with the rain. And although she could not hear the conversation between the two men, as the thunder kept booming the whole time, she received the distinct impression that the stranger's voice was only slightly less deep and rumbling. She watched her father usher him inside and quickly ran back to her chamber, fearful lest her spying should be detected.

The stranger stayed for a week. During this time, she politely greeted the men in the morning, and stayed in her chamber all day, although for courtesy's sake she was forced to join them for their evening meal. She learned that the stranger was a rich count, travelling far to settle some legal business, and that his bearing and wealth had impressed her father. Each night, once the meal was cleared, and at the old man's insistence, cards were procured, and a fresh bottle of wine was plonked down onto the wooden table. The young woman sat there, bored senseless but too polite to move, as her father squandered the remains of her inheritance. Silently she gazed across the table, imploring the count to rise from his seat and end the game, willing him to understand that her father was a sick man. But the count doggedly continued to play, a slight smile twisting the corners of his mouth, his hands brushing across the cards like swallow wings. The count only took his eyes off the cards to snatch a glimpse of her face, after

which he would look down again and gamble like a man possessed. She knew then that he would not stop until her father had nothing.

Soon the final night came. The candles fluttered and smoked on the hearth, a cold draft whirled around the drawing room, and even the wine tasted bad. At the table, the cards fell against the old man with a sickening rapidity. When luck finally deserted him, it was as if bad fortune rushed in to fill the void. After losing all his gold, he played first with silver, then copper coins, and eventually thrust his dead wife's jewellery down onto the table. Still the cards turned against him. Looking around feverishly, he twisted a ring off his wizened finger, and threw down his own wedding band. It landed on the table with a dull tinkle, rolling in a circle like a severed head.

When the last bottle was drunk, and the night sky had faded to grey, and the dim candles were all but extinguished, the old man stood up from the table. 'Sir, I must retire from our game,' he muttered in a sorrowful voice. 'It seems that I have lost more than I possess.' The count merely looked at him, and the air in the room grew heavy. The old man's heart thudded like clods of turf being thrown into a grave. The angels of the house took one look at the scene and fled, taking love with them. The girl understood that life, as she knew it, was coming to an end.

'We can continue to play,' murmured the count, voice heavy with wine. Looking at the young woman, he greedily licked his lips.

'But how?' asked the old man. His bleary eyes glistened with hope, and he straightened his hunched back, bent like a bow by a thousand card games. 'What can I wager? I have nothing left!' His eyes frantically scanned

the room, searching for some last treasure that he could stake. Anything would do.

'I'll play for what's at your right hand,' said the count, stroking his chin. Confused, the old man looked around, seeing nothing to his right except his beloved daughter. Glancing at the wall behind her, he saw nothing of value; as for his daughter, she wore no jewellery – and as he well knew, neither was there coin in her purse. When realisation dawned, like an axe slicing deep into green wood, he guiltily clutched his grey beard. But like all gamblers, he knew that luck would return with the next hand, and that he was sure to win everything back in a single glorious coup. He would buy his daughter new gowns, their house would shine with polished plate, the holes in the roof would be replaced by fresh shingles, and fat horses would whicker and prance in the stables. His friends would return, he would pay everyone back two-fold – nay, he'd pay them three times what he owed! – townspeople would once again call for tea, and even his dead wife would walk smiling through the front door.

The cards ruffled and fell onto the table in a tiny series of clicks. There was a flicking noise as the count dealt, the slow swoon as the cards were gathered up by the players and rustled into neat fans. The old man leant forward, expecting victory, so strong was the hand he had been dealt. The count moved closer to the table, forehead furrowed with concentration, the smell of sweat smoking from his garments. He lay down his cards, his gentleman's manners cast aside, and impatiently gestured for the old man to reveal his hand. With trembling fingers, the father's cards dropped onto the table like stones.

Of course, he lost.

Early the next morning, before sunrise, the count ushered the daughter into his waiting coach, fearful that the old man would renege on his deal. As the coach bumped off down the road, the girl watched her childhood home become smaller and smaller and finally vanish into the distance. Although she owned nothing except the faded gown she wore, and a battered trunk full of similar garments, and although she barely knew this man sitting beside her, the young woman felt hopeful. Travel, like gambling, begets this attitude: the certain belief that things will soon improve.

She left behind her a weeping nurse and a father unable to reckon his loss. The old man finally understood what it meant to have nothing left to lose. After watching the coach until it rumbled and shuddered out of sight, he went back inside and sat down on his daughter's bed, stroking an embroidered tiger she had sewn as a child. Examining it closely, he saw a small drop of blood where she had pricked herself with a needle. The drop of blood had fallen on the golden tiger's eye, turning it a drab rust brown. Later that afternoon, shortly after lunch, the old man put on his best remaining suit and hanged himself in the stable. By the time his skin had cooled, his daughter was already many miles away.

After many days and nights of hard travel, the coach rumbled up to the door of the count's castle, and the girl settled into her new life. It was a cold country, the ground was often covered with snow, and she found it difficult to stay warm. It took some time to adjust to the unexpected luxury of new gowns, enough food on the table, and a roof that didn't leak. Every night the count would come to their chamber, pull off her clothing as if she was nothing more than a husk of corn, and take his pleasure. He found with satisfaction that everything was as it should be: his new bride was both modest and chaste, deferring to his tastes, and exhibiting a pleasing submission throughout the sexual act. During the day, the count would hunt or visit neighbouring gentry, harass his business manager, or dabble in horse breeding. Left alone, the young woman would sit by the fire and sew. Like so many newly married couples, the count quickly became gently bored with his wife.

I roll over in the bed and press my belly into the white sheets. 'Will you stroke my back?' I ask the manservant, and he complies, measuring his slow strokes so they underscore the rhythm of his words. I lie there, eyes closed, the simple pleasures of touch and words dissolving the tension in my shoulders. 'Is that good?' he whispers. 'Yes,' I reply, 'but please continue your story.'

A few weeks later, a huge full moon rose in the eastern sky. Its silver light was so bright that the sandstone walls of the castle turned canary yellow, and the moat appeared to be made of molten silver. The young bride persuaded her husband to drink a great deal of wine, fetching him glass after glass of the thick red wine that she knew that he loved, the stuff that tastes of furrowed mud and ancient trees, and sweetly stroked his brow. Well before midnight, the servants had to carry him to his chamber, so deep was his intoxication. The count woke late the next morning to find his beautiful young wife sleeping beside him, her lips parted and her lolling tongue rose-red.

The next month it was the same, and the next and the next. Eventually the count became curious about this monthly pattern. Stricken with jealousy at the thought that his wife may be harbouring a secret lover, he prepared a cunning trap to unveil her deceit. He secretly

exchanged the bottles of wine with blackberry juice, and when the full moon came, pretended to drink his fill, acting the part of a drunk with gusto. As his voice slurred, and his touch became lecherous, the young woman smiled, stroked his brow, and continued to ply him with yet more wine. Peering out from under his brows, he was amazed by the silent efficiency of her movements, the intelligence lurking behind her eyes. After pretending to pass out on the dining table, he let the servants carry him to their chamber, where he lay still on the bed.

From the moment the door closed behind the last servant, his wife was a different person. She hurried towards him like a nurse, lifted first one eyelid and then another, quickly checked his penis (which was soft), raised and let fall one leaden arm after the other. Basically, she did everything she could to ascertain that her husband was dead drunk. Then she walked over to the fire and turned her back to the bed. Stretching slim arms overhead, she pulled off first her gown, then her corset and petticoat, finally stockings, slippers, and lace underclothes. Silhouetted against the fire, with his eyes half closed, all he could see was the outline of her lithe form and long legs as, surprisingly, she wriggled out of yet another layer. Feeling himself stiffen, for his wife was an unusually lovely person, the count gulped down a mouthful of fresh saliva.

The slight sound was enough to alert his companion. She swiftly turned and paced over to the bed, leaned over him and took a deep sniff. The count felt something warm and furry twist against his thigh, long hairs tickle against his face. He lay as still as the dead, keeping his breathing regular, letting a tiny rivulet of drool cascade from the corner of his mouth. Satisfied, she stalked over to the window, and flinging it open, leapt out into the light of the full moon and was gone.

The count jumped up and rushed towards the window. He could see nothing but the blazing light of the moon and the black shadows of the trees. In the distance was the hoarse cry of some animal, a thud, then all was silent. A sudden chill seized his heart and he huddled close to the fire. And then he saw it. Lying in a small pile on the hearth, still warm and smelling of her perfume, was an entire human skin. Picking it up, he observed the flaps of his wife's breasts dangling from the chest, her long legs, empty of flesh, hanging like stockings, and her glorious hair crumpled into a hollow bird's nest.

All night the count paced back and forwards in the chamber, unable to decide what to do, terrified if his wife should return, unwilling to accept the evidence in front of his eyes. Just before dawn, in the blackest part of the night, he heard a noise outside the window. Quickly he threw himself onto the bed and pretended to sleep. Through slitted eyes he saw his wife leap in through the window, graceful as a cat. She stretched and yawned, revealing a row of delicately pointed teeth. Aghast, he lay frozen on the bed and watched as she picked up the human skin, climbing into it as if it were the supplest leather coat. Smoothing the skin into place and adjusting the scalp so that her hairline started in the right place – neither too low nor too high – she pulled on the fingers like they were gloves and rolled up the leg skin as if it were stockings. When she turned away from the firelight, she was once again human.

Although her husband thought he would never sleep, somehow he nodded off. He woke late the next morning to find his wife lying beside him. Scarcely able to believe what had happened, he reached over and poked her

shoulder. Woken by the touch, she looked at him with her big blue eyes and quietly enquired, 'My husband, may I fetch you some breakfast?'

And so, things went between them. The count said nothing of what he had seen that night, fearing that his mind was weak and that madness would soon destroy him. Thoroughly unnerved, he watched his wife carefully, hoping for even the slightest evidence of her midnight transformation. But he watched in vain, for his wife continued her irreproachable life as an ideal partner, sitting beside the castle fireplace, busy hands darting like swallows as she embroidered golden finches onto a piece of orange silk.

The following month, when the moon was full, he gathered his courage and again played the part of the drunk. Carried to his bedchamber by loyal servants, through half-shut eyes he watched as his wife shed her human skin and leapt from the chamber window. All that night, he listened closely to the sounds of animals hunting outside, and knew that in the morning, a trail of dead things would be found in the surrounding paddocks. His heart beat louder and louder as he waited for the dawn to arrive.

At the blackest part of the night, when most souls die, and the heavens are crowded with the recently departed, there was a rustling outside the bedroom window. Taken aback, the count remained standing by the fire, prepared to meet his fate. Something large leapt in through the window, landed gracefully, and then stood up tall to face him. As it moved out of the shadows, he had never been more terrified, for the creature walking towards him was scarcely recognisable as his wife. It was covered in striped fur, with a long tail that twitched like an angry serpent, blazing feline eyes and small folded ears. A tiger's face where her beautiful countenance should have been, long claws thrust from her white fingertips. Whiskers quivered on her smooth cheeks, furry velvet breasts emerged from the magnificent arch of her rib cage, she reeked of green smoke and hot urine. Walking straight past him, she leapt onto the bed, landing on all fours, and he caught a glimpse of her cunt, the pale pink slit of a virgin pearl.

The sight of his wife, the tiger, lying prone on their bed, her sex raised and long tail twitching like a hooked eel unsettled the count more than it is possible to express. Staggering forward, almost paralysed with shock, he did the only thing he could think of: he unbuttoned his flies and rammed his cock into the waiting slit. And so it was that the count and his tiger bride made love with a savagery and a fire he had never known. As she raked him with her long claws, the man felt warm fur and animal muscles encase his member, stiff whiskers grinding into his face, febrile leather pads press against his papery human skin. With a tail twisted around his thighs, and claws clamped to his back, he tasted paradise. In the morning, waking with his wife, human once again, he felt destitute, wanting nothing more than this exquisite pain.

After this night, every month was the same. While his human wife gave no acknowledgement of her animal self, sitting with lowered head as she sewed by the fire, the count felt her watching him with living eyes; silently they waited for the next full moon. On the nights when the moon filled half the sky, they retired early to their chamber. She would throw off her human skin, and leaping out the window, return hours later covered with the blood of other beasts. Then they would mate like savage animals. Although in the morning, his body was covered with dangerous welts, deep jagged gashes, he grew to crave these exchanges and longed for their monthly embrace. Soon he became obsessed with the moon, watching it every night, aching for the next lunar flood.

One evil day, desperately wanting to see his tiger bride, and bored with his perfect human partner, he devised a plan to trap his wife in her tiger skin. Not realising what a good hand he had been dealt, the count dreamed of caging his tiger bride. He smiled at the thought of her wearing a collar and muzzle, chained to the iron bars of a large enclosure, a slave to his every desire. His grin broadened as he imagined the pleasure of clipping her long claws. He imagined the intense pleasure of thrusting his cock into her muzzled mouth, of pushing into a hairy anus, of ejaculating on the short fur of those velvety breasts. Mouth wet with desire, he waited anxiously for the night to arrive.

The full moon rose, flooding the castle windows like a second sun. Dogs howled and the lunatics of the region lifted broken voices to join the chorus. The count and his wife, as was their habit, retired early to their chamber. He stood by the fire as she ripped off her clothes then squirmed out of her human skin. Dropping to all fours, she leapt from the chamber window, thick haunches bulging in the silver moonlight. Soon the night was silent, save for the muffled sounds of her bloody hunt.

With gleeful anticipation, the count grabbed her human skin and hurled it into the fire. Time seemed to slow as he watched the pink skin fly through the air, breast flaps joggling, fingers splayed like stars, long legs akimbo. At the last moment, he almost reached out to catch the skin. He almost pulled it from the fire where it had landed with a wet stinging hiss. He nearly grabbed a poker and raked the mound of soft flesh away from the hot flames.

But he did none of these things, so determined was he to possess his tiger bride, to control her body, to enjoy complete mastery of her wild being. There was the smell of smoking bacon, fat sputtering; the breast flaps quickly crisped and jumped about in a series of small explosions, a pool of heavy yellow liquid ran from the hearth. There was an explosion, then a sudden flat feeling as if the world had stopped turning. Smoke poured from the skin, rolling across the room like giant storm clouds. Outside the moon dived behind a cloud and everything went black. Enveloped in the thick smoke, the count collapsed senseless on the floor. And so the night passed.

He woke to find his human bride lying beside him, solicitously stroking his head, her blue eyes irreproachable. 'Shall I fetch you some coffee?' she enquired in her soft voice. And he knew then that the tiger was gone forever. Turning his face towards the pillow, so thoughtfully placed under his head, he wept until he had no tears left.

'Do you want me to continue?' asks the manservant. 'It is nearly morning.'

'Yes,' I murmur, entranced, burrowing my face into the pillow. 'I want to know what happens next.' He eases the sheet covering my back and with long strokes, caresses the skin from the back of my neck to the base of my spine. Feeling his fingers brush the crack in my behind, I arch my back slightly, willing his hands to move lower, but to no avail: he was born to serve men, not to master women.

Time passed and though neither of them spoke of it, the destruction of the tiger hung between them like the death of a child. Sitting frozen by the fire, the count gazed sorrowfully at his wife, while she watched her hands flicker across the surface of her embroidery. All wildness vanished, as if it had never been. Their waists thickened, food tasted like ashes and sand, sex was light without shadows: the polite insertion of tepid flesh into an accommodating hole. By day the count played the part of the affable aristocrat, but at night he ached for his animal other.

One dismal morning, unable to bear his mistake or the sight of his human wife any longer, the count saddled a horse and rode away from the castle. He had not gone far when he spotted a travelling menagerie meandering along the road ahead. Spurring his horse, he quickly overtook the caravan. 'Hold hard!' he called to the lead rider. 'Do you have any tigers?' The leader stroked his chin, and then admitted that yes, the caravan had been blessed with three big cats. 'I will give you fifty pieces of gold if you let me look at them; but you must leave me alone with them,' cried the count. The sight of the gold soon convinced the man, and so the caravan withdrew. The count was left alone with a cage full of wild tigers.

As soon as the caravan was out of sight, the count pushed himself against the bars, reaching through them to try and fondle the big cats. The tigers drew back, scenting the madness of this creature, appalled by his lack of fear. 'It is me,' he cried plaintively to the female cat, 'your husband. Do you not recognise me?' Seeing no response, no spark of recognition, he wrenched open the cage door and threw himself inside with a ringing cry of, 'Beloved!' It was to be his last word. The male tiger pounced, slicing his throat open with a single kiss, while the other cats snapped his limbs and ripped his torso apart like cotton. In less than a minute the count's body lay in fifty pieces on the cage floor. (Fifty pieces of gold for fifty pieces of flesh: wisely do the prophets say 'be careful what you wish for').

The following morning the weeping bride sent for the priest, explaining that her husband had suddenly sickened and died. And so it was that the count was able to have a decent burial, his reputation intact, shielded from the ignominy of his true end. You can still visit the village where he is buried. On his tomb someone has scrawled the following inscription: 'Do not cage what you have no right to keep'.

Power

When I wake the next morning, I find myself alone in the Sultan's bed. The feeling is so peculiar as to be overwhelming. Lying there, I try to remember how many nights have passed since I arrived at his palace. I used to keep a record, a piece of paper scratched with dates, but now I am no longer sure. I think it has been about a thousand, maybe more, perhaps less. I roll over and bury my face into the pillow, in the hollow where his head had rested, luxuriating in the scent, letting my limbs kick across the clean cotton sheets.

A discreet cough startles me. The manservant is hovering near the door, holding a steaming basin of water and a towel. Something in the stiffness of his spine makes me gather a sheet around myself, protecting my body, shielding my nudity. He slides into the room, carefully places the basin on the table next to the bed, and quickly departs. A few seconds later an ancient man ambles into the room. His spine is hunched like a winter tree and he has a long white beard as sharp as a spear. I feel my blood grow cold: this is the Grand Vizier.

History tells us that in the court of many Sultans, there is a man who stands behind the throne, often more bloodthirsty and ruthless than his master: manipulative, cunning and deeply political. And so it is in this court, too. I had heard whispered stories about the Sultan's Grand Vizier but had never met him. From the frozen expressions of my servants, I understood that fear greets his every move. People say he is so old that, as a grown man, he advised the Sultan's grandfather. On first meeting you would describe him as a charming old gentleman, perhaps a bit doddery, good-natured and affable, perhaps an academic. With subsequent meetings or close contact, this impression quickly evaporates; he is as cruel as razor wire. He arranges the palace courtiers like pawns, plays favourites, unexpectedly reverses his benevolence, leaving the fallen one to wonder, search for reasons, fear for their life. Smiling and nodding, he comes towards me. An icy trickle of sweat squiggles its way down my naked spine.

The Grand Vizier gently seats himself on the side of the bed, much closer than I would like, an unholy smirk peeling thin pink lips from his pointed yellow teeth. His long beard brushes my knees as he begins to speak. 'You must be Scheherazade, my dear, the young woman of whom I've heard so much.' He reaches forward and pats my knee, squeezing it, his eyes lifeless, the old hand scrabbling like an animal's strong claws. The claw moves upwards, navigating the firm flesh of my thigh; I lower my head, unable to bear his touch, but sensing the absolute danger of this beast. His hand stops inches from my pubis and remains there, the tight grip intensifying, an unmoving stare and that awful grimace. Then he reaches over and pushes my head up so he looks directly into my face. Eyes vacant as a child's marbles, he pauses to scan my red lips, flushed cheeks,

dark eyes and long white neck. He gives a small courtly bow. 'You are as beautiful as reported…' The compliment freezes the air and hangs there like a dagger, nothing disguising the threat that it represents. Unable to tolerate his gaze, I again drop my head, unwilling to face him, wanting to disappear.

He sniffs, having assessed his prey, makes a decision and stands up. When the old man speaks again, his voice is conversational and light. Walking casually around the Sultan's bedchamber, his eyes snatch what they can from the scene. He wanders over to the leather contraption, gives it a contemptuous push, and sneers as the silver chains jingle. Turning back to face me, his eyes are like endless night.

'There have been many girls like you,' he states. His voice is matter-of-fact, a casual observer could even describe the tone as kind; the combination is excruciating. 'Just before you arrived there was an especially beautiful one, a blonde from the northern islands. The Sultan's soldiers found her wandering on the coast, near one of their wrecked boats, quite distraught, and brought her here.' He pauses to let his works take effect, stroking his spear of a beard, pretending to reflect. 'We had never seen anything like her. She had straight blonde hair that fell down to her ankles, spoke not a word of our language, but that didn't seem to bother the Sultan,' he adds, face breaking into a knowing leer. 'She had some strange habits: I remember watching her swim naked in an outdoor pool, the one in the walled courtyard. Her long hair hung down like a silk curtain. She made no attempt to cover her body, was perfectly at ease in her own skin. And why would she cover herself? She was sublime.'

He looked down his aquiline nose at me, his expression communicating that by comparison, I was nothing more than a cheap whore, and an ugly one at that. 'She lasted six weeks before the Sultan cut off her pretty head.' Moving towards the door, he turned to spit out one final piece of poison, 'I think her name was Olga.'

When he finally leaves, my world turns black. I curl up on the Sultan's bed in a foetal position and shiver uncontrollably. I cannot get warm, no matter how many blankets I pull over myself, no matter how much I chafe my icy skin. Coldness pierces my heart, spreading little arrows of freezing pain along my limbs. Olga. Like actors rehearsing a scene, again and again I imagine the Sultan walking into the walled courtyard; in front of him stands a naked blonde, her hair a waterfall of wet silk. She turns to him and smiles, glorious in her innocence, her nakedness as natural as the sky. The thought of the Sultan, my Sultan, bending her over and piercing her with his thick cock, her face crumpled with exquisite pain, dark and light bodies intertwined. Olga. I moan and stick my thumb in my mouth, finding comfort in the childhood habit of sucking, knowing that my shivering will not stop. When a second wave of pain arrives, it brings bitter knowledge with it. A truth even more terrible than jealousy: the futile hatred of a dead rival. Even Olga, the golden-haired Scandinavian beauty, was unable to escape the Sultan's knife.

Fall

I am sick for days. Tended day and night by the manservant, and the blonde maid with the unremarkable face, I lack the strength to continue living yet find myself too indifferent for death. It is as if the universe has been bled dry of colour, leaving this pallid void of grey despair, a washed-up landscape populated by liars and thieves, all humans scavenging creatures of the lowest motive. The Grand Vizier's poison works its evil spell. Food loses its taste, my skin becomes as dry and cracked as the desert, lifting a cup to my lips seems an intolerable effort. I care for nothing. When, after many nights, the Sultan does not come to visit me, I know that he has abandoned me, and my love is a sham. Like the other girls, I will end my days as meat in the mouth of caged beasts.

They send for the Sultan's physician, a wise man, respected across the land, yet he can do nothing. The physician holds my pale wrist and feels the crab scuttle of my pulse, peers into my dull eyes, obliges me to poke my furry tongue out of its stinking hole, even suffers me to let blood. Yet it is all in vain. Everything that had once made me beautiful is gone. I lie on the bed, a thin sheet of skin holding together organs that reluctantly continue to function, bones and muscles heavy with sadness, heart encased with black lead. Everything ceases to matter. Once, when I had not moved for a full day and night, I heard the servants whispering above me, their voices shrill with fear. Someone asks who would tell the Sultan if I died; as the girl's voice rises with panic, the others turn on her, urging her to be silent. 'It will not come to that,' the manservant interrupts, his quiet voice loaded with authority. They fall silent and creep from the room.

A sound of a light tread beside my bed and then the manservant is there, looking down at me. He reaches over to wipe my forehead with a damp cloth. My eyes are closed, but I listen to his breathing and understand that he is about to say something important. He hesitates, bites his lip, air puffing out in a sudden hiss. 'He has not left you,' whispers the manservant. 'He rides across the desert these many nights. There is a war between tribes to the north – they are attacking the trading caravans – and he goes there to stop it. He will come back to you,' he murmurs, stroking my hand, 'it will not be long.' He holds my hand, kisses my brow like a brother, and recites the following tale:

The Way of the Pauper

There was once an old merchant who had three clever daughters. Knowing that his time would soon come, he called the girls to him and asked them to choose their inheritance. 'Many years ago,' he gasped, 'I met an old man dying in the desert, and when I gave him a sip from my canteen, he blessed me with three wishes. I never used these wishes, wanting to save them for a rainy day, but now I give them to you.'

The eldest daughter eagerly stepped forward. She was a fine-looking woman with pride woven into the straight line of her back and the lofty tilt of her chin. 'I wish for a handsome husband!' she cried. In an instant, a suitable young man appeared in the room, desirable as the harvest moon. They were soon married. But as her pretty husband had many friends and lovers, he was out every night and day, and eventually the eldest daughter grew as sour as last season's grapes.

The middle daughter rubbed her hands together. 'I wish for a huge pile of gold!' she called. There was a slight quiver in the air, and immediately a glimmering pile of coin appeared on the rug. It was a huge amount of money. At first, she spent it very freely and attracted many fine companions, but soon her supply began to dwindle. Discovering that she lacked the skills necessary to earn any more, but having grown accustomed to a profligate lifestyle, the middle daughter grudgingly took a job as a rich lady's maid.

Finally, it was the youngest daughter's turn. She was a wistful child, prone to books, daydreaming and speaking to animals, even imagining that the latter could talk back. As the least practical of his children, she was also the merchant's favourite. The dying man patted the edge of his bed and said, 'Come here, my dear, and speak your heart's desire.' She sat, shy and downcast, twisting her fingers together, knowing that her wish would not please him.

'I want to be an artist,' she muttered.

'An artist!' he cried, but it was too late. In an instant there was magic in the room. When the girl looked up from the floor, it was as if torches were burning behind her green eyes.

When the girl looked up from the floor, it was as if torches were burning behind her green eyes.

The youngest daughter lived brilliantly for a few years, happy with her choice, glowing with the magic golden light of a soul following its true path. She told stories and painted little pictures, garnering so much fame that even in the big cities people would point and say, 'There goes the merchant's daughter, who chose art over gold.' They would marvel at such foolhardy courage and feel very glad that their own children had more sense. She took up with a musician, a handsome fellow with bad teeth, irregular as a cheap watch. Although she was very poor, it seemed to the youngest daughter that this way of life would go on forever.

Meanwhile, her stories spread across the city. Lovers told them in bed, drinkers shared them in taverns, and wise mothers placed them carefully under their tongues before putting their children to sleep at night. Beyond the walls of the city, armies carried them with their spears and shields into battle, navies sailed with them packed in the hold as precious cargo, and soon even the great ambassadors of the world – men and women who could subdue wild tigers and quell riots with a single perfectly formed syllable – would not leave home without one or two stories to pacify hostile nations.

The next winter was unusually sharp. Frost wrapped itself around every tree and ice choked the rivers. In the cemetery, the undertaker's steel pickaxe bounced off the stony dirt. Overhead little birds flew slower and slower until they finally stopped, falling out of the sky like frozen blossom. One night, unable to afford firewood, the merchant's daughter huddled in her wretched hovel. The musician had vanished with the last of her coins. With the cold wrapped around her like a woollen blanket, she went to sleep dreaming happily of art and stories, and in the morning she was quite dead.

I open my eyes and look at the manservant askance. 'What a horrible story,' I whisper. He stands up, awkwardly brushing imaginary dust from his thighs.

'Not at all,' he murmurs, moving towards the door. With the candlelight behind him, he looks like a silhouette cut from fine black paper. Then he turns towards me and with great seriousness proclaims: 'An artist may not live forever, but her art lives on.'

Return

When I awake, the grey mist has lifted slightly. I eat a light breakfast and sleep until lunch. When I wake again, the Sultan is standing by my bed watching me intently. 'How long has she been like this?' I hear him ask the manservant, who mutters a reply. 'What happened?' asks the Sultan, leaning forward to glare at my cavernous face, his eyes glimmering with rage. Then the mist rises again, and I drift back into my painless void, the glimpse of his black eyes both wonderful and terrible. I dream and once more the ghostly figure of Olga haunts my unconscious. In a recurring sequence of images, I see her push open the carved gate of a secret courtyard, pull her dress over her head, and wade naked into a pond full of flowers, her blonde hair trailing behind her in a great cape.

Then the mist rises again, & I drift back into my painless void, the glimpse of his black eyes both wonderful & terrible.

Sometimes in the dream she floats on her back, looking up at the blue sky, enjoying the heat bouncing off the high walls of the courtyard. And sometimes she is walking towards me, her mouth opening, about to say something; water beads on her splendid breasts and runs down towards the pale triangle of down framed by her strong thighs. Again and again, her mouth opens, but I cannot hear what she says. Each time she repeats herself she becomes more impatient, and frustrated hands flutter towards her mouth. 'I can't hear you,' I say in the dream, and she tries again, opening and closing her mouth like a stranded fish. 'I'm sorry, but I can't hear you...'

Muse

Somewhere in the timeless chasm after midnight, a woman's bell-like voice chants in my head. I am not entirely sure if it is a vision, or perhaps the manservant stroking my head and reciting another tale, but I wake with these words running through my mind, cold and clear as a mountain stream:

There was once an artist who loved to make paper cuts. She sat in her studio all day long, snipping away industriously at white paper with a sharp blade, leaving piles of offcuts on the wooden floor. Soon the offcuts looked like small mounds of snow. She did not like to be disturbed while she was working and would sing to herself as she crafted scenes of great beauty and enchantment: ice castles frozen among the clouds, reindeer with horns as big as flowering chestnut trees, and winter sparrows with bright red hearts that shone through the thin skin of their breasts.

She liked to make pictures of wolves, white peacocks, and snow leopards, and once even attempted the terribly difficult shape of a kangaroo. It turned out ok, but when she showed it to the people in her village, nobody believed that the long tail and the tiny front legs were real. Regardless, she continued in her quest for the perfect paper cut.

One afternoon, when the artist was gathering firewood in the woods, she came across an owl sitting on a tree branch. This was quite odd, as it was still early, with the sun only just beginning to dip through the leaves overhead. What was even stranger was that this was a talking owl. It bent over its branch, looked at her thoughtfully with dazzling golden eyes, and asked her a simple question. 'Where do you get your inspiration?'

The artist looked at the owl, and the owl looked at the artist, and neither of them spoke for a moment. It was the same question that the artist had been asked many times by people in her village, and she never knew how to respond. 'I'm really not sure,' said the artist, 'ideas just come to me.' The owl nodded thoughtfully, rotated its head, blinked three times, and flew away. The artist gathered some twigs and fallen pine branches and returned to her studio. As she stood outside the door, juggling her armful of tinder, she heard an odd tapping and ticking sound coming from within.

Opening the door, she was greeted by the incredible sight of her little paper cuts dancing around the room. A white peacock was strutting across the fireplace mantle, tail raised high, so that she could see the blue wall through the decorative holes in its feathers. A wolf and a snow leopard wrestled on the floor, tearing shreds of confetti off each other. And even the kangaroo was bouncing excitedly from table to floor and back again. She screamed, dropped her firewood, and fled.

The next day the artist, unsure of what else to do, went to find the owl. She searched the forest until sundown, and finally the bird appeared, perched like a king on the low hanging branch of a silver birch. 'The paper cuts,' she stuttered. 'They've come to life!' The owl looked mildly bored. It preened and puffed its chest feathers like a visiting academic.

'Why are the paper cuts dancing around my studio?'
she asked.

'Imagination brings ideas to life,' said the owl smugly.
'Everyone knows that.'

The artist stared blankly at the owl. 'But what's that got
to do with inspiration?' she asked.

'Art inspires art, and artists inspire other artists,' the
owl droned, gripping the branch. The artist waited as it
arranged its leg tufts, snapping the fluffy feathers into
neat little fans. 'You are beholden to both artists you
know and artists you will never meet, in an invisible
chain that spans the centuries. But please
remember the many artists who have been prevented
from practising their craft, and honour their lives.' And
with that, the owl nodded its head magisterially and
flew off into the darkening sky. It flew so high that soon
its white feathers looked like a silver comet dancing
among the clouds.

The artist returned home to her studio. Approaching the
door, she was encouraged by the silence within. Peeping
inside, she was astonished to find a large papercut of
intricate design hanging on the wall over her fireplace.
A circular paper cut, with a peaceable kingdom of many
fine animals and a snow-covered mountain in the background. And in the centre of the design, a tiny picture of
a naked woman with long blonde hair looking in a mirror,
and in its reflection, my own face.

Cure

The next day a little more of the colour had leached back into the world. I lift a glass to my own lips and drink, noting the rich red sweetness of the liquid. The manservant props me up on pillows and I look out at the sky, still caring for nothing, but wondering if I will see a bird fly past. It is strange to spend an entire morning waiting for a wild bird's flight. At midday there is a knock at the door and the manservant ushers in another famous physician, an elderly man with a kind face. Like a hen shaping her nest, he settles himself into the comfortable chair next to my bed. I know, even before he opens his mouth, that this guy is a talker. I imagine his wife sending him to the morning market to buy fruit and him returning at sundown, having spoken at length to every traveller, friend, stranger, and business associate he met along the way. As it is, my instincts are proved correct.

The physician starts by telling me his name, that he has known the Sultan for years, what a lovely man, treated him for toothache when the Sultan was a child, but not a single problem since: such health! Such a remarkable constitution! Then he moves onto my medical condition. He says that he had been to see the Sultan's physician, who could find nothing physically wrong with me, so they both agreed that the problem must lie in the soul. 'Or the heart,' he whispers conspiratorially, giving me a wink. Despite myself, I find myself liking him, and wink back.

As it is a matter of the soul, he says, he has come here today not to minister to me with physic, but to tell me a story, for stories feed the soul as surely as bread fills the stomach. And besides, even if both physicians were wrong, and the problem lurked within my body, I would still have heard a cracking good yarn. What did I think of that? I tell him that I thought it was a very fine idea, that I love stories, and raise my body up on the pillows so I could be more comfortable, smiling with anticipation.

The physician straightens his back and clears his throat. I laugh privately to myself, observing that he had been trained in the classical manner of declamation, a manner of delivery at least fifty years out of fashion. Then, in a voice as rich as beef gravy (gravy, that is, from cracked heifer thigh bones, boiled for three days, leaving only a rich silt of fat and salt clinging to the bottom of an iron pan) and with his humorous countenance suddenly extinguished, he recounts the following tale. This is the physician's story:

The Tale of the White Peacock

There was once a powerful king who lived in a castle on a rock on a mountain in a land far, far away. The mountain was so high that the roads that led to the castle gates zig-zagged up through snow and ice, and quite often, when the weather became especially cold, clouds would form a halo around the castle's towers and the mountain animals would tap at the palace door, wordlessly asking the guard if they may come in and rest by a fire. On a winter's evening, it was not unusual to find a snow leopard, bear and wolf calmly sharing a circle of warmth in front of the kitchen fire.

One night, when it was so cold that birds fell dead from the sky, and icicles crusted everyone's eyelashes, the palace guard heard a tap-tap-tapping at the palace gate. 'It is too late,' he yelled, thinking that it was a wolf at the door (for the snow leopard and bear had already taken their usual places by the fire). 'Come back in the morning.' Now it was not that the palace guard was a hard-hearted man, far from it, but on this particular evening his sweetheart had come to call, and the cold had made her friendlier than usual. So he wanted to waste no time, in case his brief departure caused her passion to freeze again.

Tap-tap-tap, came the noise again, and the guard tried to ignore it; his sweetheart sat astride him, her plump hands clamped to his ginger sideburns as she sucked his tongue, but there it came again, tap-tap-tap, like a little hammer on the inside of his skull. Tap-tap-tap ... tap-tap-tap... 'I'm coming!' he bawled, dumping the girl off his lap, face scarlet with frustration. He rushed towards the palace door, trembling with anger, ready to give the wolf a piece of his mind. As he ran, he composed an incendiary list of insults: 'You miserable, flea-ridden, offal eating, stinking pile of maggot dung, how dare you...' But when he opened the door, all these words flew straight out of his mind, and were lost in the snowflakes whirling outside, for there on the doorstep was a most unusual creature. A white peacock stood trembling in the snow.

'Here, Salona,' he called back over his shoulder, 'come and have a look at this.' Then it was his sweetheart's turn to stamp to the door, muttering under her breath,

'Oh, you poor fool, who would choose a stinking wolf over a fine pair of ta-tas like these?' Though when she too beheld the white peacock, she became uncharacteristically silent, so rare was this particular bird. 'Oooohhhh,' they both chorused in unison, standing back as the peacock proudly shook snow crystals off his pearly tail and sauntered into the warm antechamber. He seemed to be asking, as clearly as a human would, which way to the kitchen fire?

'Come this way,' urged the guard, leading the way and occasionally looking back over his shoulder at his strange new guest. 'You'll find it lovely and warm in here. Err, sorry about the wait, won't happen again.' The red-haired Salona brought up the rear, a white peacock stalked along with head held high, and the stooped guard muttered his apologies. What a strange procession they made.

The guard held open the kitchen door and in walked the peacock, heading straight for the fire, and for the first time Salona noticed that the bird's legs were frozen blue. 'Oh, you poor thing!' she exclaimed, bustling forward to fill a dish with hot water, 'You're nearly dead with cold.' The snow leopard and the bear took one look at the peacock and seemed to shrink to half their size, automatically backing away to offer the bird the warmest position in front of the fire. Salona put the dish of steaming water on the floor and the peacock stood in it, soaking his frozen feet. Placing a dish of seed close to the fire, and with respectfully amazed looks, Salona and the guard backed out of the room with a final chorus of, 'If you need anything else – anything at all – we're just next door.' A few seconds later the guard returned, ushering in a sheepish-looking wolf. 'A latecomer,' he explained, shutting the door behind him. Finally, the animals were alone.

'I'm sorry I'm late,' muttered the wolf, looking down at his paws and giving them an unnecessary lick, 'bloody awful weather.' Other than shooting him a brief chilling glare, the peacock chose to ignore him.

The bird looked around, drew himself upright, and in an upper-crust English accent declared, 'I now call this meeting to session. Any apologies?'

'Ollie couldn't make it, Guv,' replied the bear, 'got himself shot by a hunter last winter.'

'A minute's silence, then, for our friend and esteemed colleague Oliver the Siberian Otter.' The animals stood mute, looking at the floor, while a clock in the corner of the kitchen ticked loudly. 'Ahem,' said the peacock, clearing his throat, 'regrettable as Oliver's absence is, we do need to move on with this evening's program.'

The door creaked open again, and this time Salona entered, smiling brightly as she chattered to herself. 'I just remembered that there's some stale bread in the oven. It will make a nice meal for you, poor bird, soaked in a bit of milk.' The animals resumed their dumb stances while the good-natured woman moved around the kitchen like a dervish. 'Nearly done,' she called over the shoulder, mashing at the bread with first a spoon, then a fork and finally a blunt knife. 'All done,' she concluded brightly, the dish landing with a harsh clatter at the peacock's feet. The kitchen door crashed shut behind her.

The snow leopard looked disgusted. 'We're going to have to find a better place to meet,' he said, looking angrily towards the door. 'If they would just let us in and make themselves scarce, perhaps it would work, but not all this banging and crashing about. How are we supposed to work? I'm an artist, you know, I'm sensitive to these kinds of disruptions, they impact my creative process. I find it difficult to...' The peacock cut him off. Over the years the entire group had heard rather a lot about the snow leopard's artistic temperament, rather more than they had ever wished to know, and tolerance had worn thin.

'Yes, quite right, quite right. Now, William,' turning expectantly towards the wolf, 'do you have something that you'd like to share?'

The wolf, if it was possible, seemed to grow even smaller than before. Nervously he grinned, licking his lips with a long pink tongue, and making little kneading movements with his front paws.

'Well, I do have something, but I'm not sure– that is to say, I don't know if it's ready. That's why I was late tonight, making some last minute changes, not sure if it flows...' Still disappointed that he had been unable to wax lyrical on the engrossing subject of his creative temperament, the snow leopard perked up.

'I can take your place if you like,' he volunteered, 'it just so happens that I have something prepared.'

'Actually,' snapped the peacock, determined to maintain his authority, and raising his magnificent tail, 'I seem to remember that you read first last time. And the time before. We shall wait for William to read his piece. Don't worry, William,' he added magisterially, in an avuncular stage whisper that everyone could hear. 'We're all writers. We know it's only a draft. I'm sure it will be much better when you're finished.'

William, pale by now and trembling, lurched forward and positioned himself next to the snow leopard who, sniffing the wolf's perspiration, gave an almost imperceptible shrug, lifted his eyebrows and tried to catch the bear's eye. Failing to do so, he resumed his elaborate sulking. 'It's a poem,' the wolf gasped, 'haiku. But it doesn't comply with the traditional rule of seventeen syllables divided over three lines of five, seven and five.' He paused for breath, looking terrified. 'It's called *Wolf*. Like I said, I'm not sure if it's any good. But here goes.' Sucking in a breath that clattered in his throat like a rock avalanche, William closed his eyes and solemnly intoned:

An aching heart

Colours the moon

Deep orange tonight.

There was a brief silence in the room, then everyone spoke at once. 'Oh! Well done, William, well done!' applauded the bear, rushing forward to deliver a mighty slap on the wolf's back. The wolf winced and then smiled shyly.

Meanwhile the snow leopard, looking trenchant, merely squeezed out a polite grimace and in a cultured voice began, 'Yes, I can see what you were trying to do with the second line...' 'Jolly good!' exclaimed the peacock, beating his wings vigorously together, while the bear chorused, 'Hear him, hear him.' The snow leopard inspected the pad of one paw, trying hard to look interested, and as the animals continued to congratulate the wolf, appeared to be lost in thought. When the clapping had died down, he slowly raised his head and made eye contact with William. A strange chill entered the room, a coldness that kills camaraderie, an icy tension that even the roaring wood fire could not disperse.

'Yes,' said the snow leopard, his voice clear and crisp, 'that was quite wonderful!' The wolf smiled warmly and hung his head with pride, unused to praise from such an unexpected quarter. 'Remarkable,' went on the snow leopard, 'stunning...' The wolf looked up briefly, anxiously, and his grin began to fade. 'Just brilliant,' continued the snow leopard, voice husky and false as a blue pearl. The wolf froze, his body tense, kneading the floor with small jerking movements of his paws. 'It was, of course, a little derivative. When I think of the haiku of Kobayashi Issa...', he paused to quote the master:

Deer licking

First frost

From each other's coats.

'Well, when I think of that, your own achievement becomes that much ... braver. So well done, William. It's so much part of what this writing circle is all about, coming together and sharing drafts, the more experienced writers mentoring the less gifted. And I thought it was really sweet that you wrote something about that thing you had with that female wolf last summer. I can't remember her name, but you know the one I mean, she had a rather ugly tail ... I mean, I know it didn't last very long, I could never see what you saw in her, but goodness, she certainly gave you the seed of a good idea, didn't she?'

During the snow leopard's speech, the wolf had dropped his head to stare stoically at the floor, as if some brilliant new truth would soon flower up through the cobble-stones. But when the leopard mentioned the female wolf, he raised his head, and the hairs on the back of his neck crept up with the sullen force of sea urchin spikes. The other animals, never having seen the wolf's raised hackles before, drew back in horror. But the snow leopard, intent on the destruction of his chief literary foe, carried on without noticing. 'Yes, I could never un-derstand a tail like that,' he added with a playful laugh, 'all furry and misshapen. If I had such an appendage, I'd just hide in a cave all day! However, we snow leopards always have wonderful tails, it's one of the many physical advantages we possess...'

There was a low growl from the other side of the room, and when the snow leopard looked across, startled by the noise, he encountered the awesome sight of a snarling wolf. A full-grown adult wolf with terminal yellow eyes and dripping white fangs. A creature as lethal as it is fearless. Not surprisingly, the snow leopard quickly fell silent. The room, which had been so cosy and welcoming a few minutes earlier, became as quiet as a stone. Even the fire seemed to burn cold.

When the wolf spoke, voice deadly calm, all he said was, 'I'm good at what I do.' The words sunk into the silence like rocks plunging into a freezing pool. 'I'm good at what I do,' he repeated, standing up and walking over to the snow leopard. His face inches from the cat's face, he once more hissed the same phrase, 'I'm good at what I do.' The snow leopard crouched down, belly inches from the floor, and crawled towards the door. His long tail shivered with fear and was the last thing they saw as he vanished through the doorway. Addressing the quivering tail, rapidly receding as the leopard fled, the wolf quietly added, 'Oh, and her name was Olive. And her tail?' He smiled as he looked off into a memory only he could see, eyes bright and tongue wet. 'Her tail was wonderful...'

'My dear, I guess you're wondering what that story was all about?' asks the physician. 'Well, to tell you the truth, I'm not even sure myself. But I think it has something to do with artists needing to choose their friends wisely, always believing in themselves, and learning to work with a thousand distractions. One needs to think of the future. Art is a precious gift, my dear girl, it would be a pity to squander it.' And with that, the old physician stands up, gives me a radiant smile that crinkles his kind eyes, and walks out of my life. Hope returns to my body like a rising tide.

Gift

The next day I am stronger. The first thing I see in the morning is a large white cotton sheet covering some huge bell-shaped object, standing right in the middle of my room. I climb out of bed, my legs thin and weak, and approach the strange object. Lifting the cotton sheet, I discover a giant birdcage with slim golden bars, intricate curlicues adorning the base and curved dome. Inside a hundred finches are flying hither and thither, their plumage so bright that I have to squint to look at them. I glimpse tiny scarlet birds with vivid blue heads, feathered specks of emerald green with mustard yellow wings, sleek black bodies with minute cream spots and red wing bars, pure white finches with pink beaks and an orange species with scarlet toes. Individually, they would have been pretty: together they are magnificent.

Someone is hovering at my side. It is the manservant, looking pleased and quietly excited. 'It is a present from my master,' he explains. 'I heard you tell the first physician that you felt as if the world had lost all its colour, so we thought that you may like these birds. They're very colourful, aren't they?' He is smiling nervously, chattier than usual. I have the feeling that the finches were his idea, hesitantly suggested to the Sultan.

'They're perfect,' I reassure him, touching his arm, 'please thank your master and tell him that I love them.' A boy once again, the manservant flushes with pleasure.

A week passes as my mind and body begin to heal. It is a slow recovery. You do not know how far down you have swum until you turn and head back towards the surface. Something in the old man's story touched me, gave me a direction to aim for. I feel light-headed and vague, knowing some important truth will soon reveal itself. Lying in bed, looking at the caged finches, I realise that I was born with everything I ever needed to navigate my own life. I am both the cause of my own misfortunes and the answer to their peculiar riddles. If there is such a thing as destiny, I know that its ribbony road starts and ends in my heart. Somewhere in the quiet, flat space between illness and death, I stop dreaming of Olga. I regain the power I was born with, the power that all women are born with, but trade away, for lies and pretty things, like animals at the market.

The Diamond Necklace Game

Once upon a time there was a princess who wanted a diamond necklace. Now this would not normally be a bother, for princesses and diamond necklaces go together like salty cheese and gherkins, but this particular princess was very, very ambitious. She wanted a necklace that circled her neck like a ring of stars, with stones so full of silver-white light that they made the moon itself look dull. It was not clear to anyone, least of all the princess herself, why she needed this necklace so badly. All she knew was that she woke up with the light from a distant galaxy dazzling her eyes and fell asleep thinking of earthbound stars twinkling against her skin.

One afternoon, as the princess was walking through the woods surrounding her palace, she came across an old woman. The old woman was sitting beside a small campfire. She'd built a rough hut from fallen branches, was busy roasting a wild hare with bitter weeds, and seemed perfectly content. A small drizzle of blue smoke spiralled up from the cooking fire and globs of yellow fat spat like angry cats as they spattered down amongst the coals. Much to the princess' surprise, the old woman made no effort to curtsy or bid her good day. Accustomed as she was to a certain nervousness among her servants and acquaintances, the princess felt mildly annoyed. She stepped forward and nudged the spit holding the rabbit with the tip of her pointed shoe, so that it almost fell into the fire.

The old woman slowly looked up. 'Did you want something, dear?' she croaked.

'I am Princess Sybil, and this is my father's land,' said the princess. 'You have no right to camp here without my permission.' The old woman leaned forward and adjusted the spit so that the rabbit was once more roasting beautifully at the heart of the flames.

'Well, Sybil, may I sleep here tonight?' she asked. 'It's pronounced "sib-belle",' snapped the princess, who was a somewhat selfish young woman and perhaps also a little lonely. 'If you want to sleep here, I expect payment of some kind.'

'I see,' said the old woman, and she sprinkled a few more herbs on the meat, poked the black kettle closer to the fire, then threw some odd-looking mushrooms into it. 'And what is your price, my lovely?'

The princess looked around at the meagre bark hut, and the battered cooking equipment, and the old woman's patched cloak. There were a pair of leather boots drying beside the fire, their worn soles thin as paper. 'I would like a diamond necklace,' she announced. 'It must be made from stones that shine so brightly that they make the brightest full moon look grey.' 'A diamond necklace,' repeated the old woman, shaking her head in wonder. She spat into the fire and wiped her nose on the sleeve of her roughly woven smock.

'And what will you do if I can't find a necklace?' she asked.

'I'll set the dogs on you,' snarled the girl, turning on her heel. 'I want it by tomorrow morning,' she called as she headed back towards the palace.

After the princess had left, the woods were once again a peaceful place. The old woman sat looking into the heart of the fire, and all the woodland animals and birds, usually so shy, crept closer and closer to the hot coals. They seemed strangely unafraid of the old woman, with a swallow landing on a branch very close to her head, rabbits nibbling at grass near her feet, and a fat lizard curling up on a flame-heated stone. A delightful red fox came and sat by the fire like a tame dog, hoping for bones, and a group of slimy salamanders dragged themselves out of a nearby pool and watched from the shelter of a large fern.

Time flowed past and then the old woman took the spit off the fire and dragged the kettle away from the coals. She tore some bones and flesh off the roasted rabbit and threw them to the fox; scattered a handful of black herbs for the swallow; even tossed a couple of mushrooms to the salamanders hiding under the fern. The animals gobbled up their treats, and the old woman ate hers, smacking her lips as the blackened skin crunched in her mouth. Finally, after everyone had eaten, the fox sidled up the woman, pressing his furry head against her skirts. And the swallow flew down from its tree and perched on her shoulder. And even the salamanders bravely waddled out from under the fern and joined her by the fire.

Powerful magic was at work in this quiet forest clearing. The old woman and the animals sat there, and nobody said a word, yet you could almost see the thoughts that were jumping from one mind to another. The campfire hissed and dwindled, its coals turning first a dark red, then a deep purple, and eventually a rich cornflower blue. The little corkscrew of smoke that had risen so prettily from the flames instead flowed out across the ground. And one by one the birds above gradually stopped their singing, so that the forest became uncannily silent. Night fell, the old woman curled up by the fire, and the fox, swallow, and salamanders disappeared back into the dark woods.

The little corkscrew of smoke that had risen so prettily from the flames instead flowed out across the ground. And one by one the birds above gradually stopped their singing, so that the forest became uncannily silent.

The following morning, the first thing the old woman saw was a hunting dog's hairy muzzle pressed up against her face. As her eyes swam into focus, she saw more large dogs snapping at their leashes nearby, with a servant holding them back. The princess stood beside them with an evil grin on her face. 'Good morning,' she said acidly. 'I do hope you slept well. Do you have my diamonds?' The old woman sat up, brushing twigs from her hair.

'Actually,' she yawned, 'I do.' And reaching into her dirty bodice, she pulled a glittering necklace from her bosom. Everyone in the clearing, even the hunting dogs, gasped and took a step back! The princess' mouth dropped open. Then she surged forward and snatched the gems.

'I sent my father's greediest merchants, his most savage soldiers and entire trading caravans across the world searching for something like this, to no avail. And yet here it is, delivered by a beggar woman in my own woods!' Just from the feel of the stones, the princess knew these diamonds were not paste. 'Where on earth did you get this?'

The old woman chuckled. 'I asked the fox,' she said, 'who is an unusually clever animal, to help me. The fox told me about huge diamonds deep in the earth, far from here, in a crevasse so deep that no human eye can see its way through the darkness. But it was too far to travel there in a single day, so he suggested that I send a flock of swallows, as they fly faster than thought. And these swallows flew through the night with a single, brave salamander clasped gently in their claws. This salamander pleaded with the army of salamanders who live in this distant crevasse, begging them to give up their most precious stones. I'm told there was some fierce haggling between this ambassador and the foreign salamanders, but eventually the latter relented and burrowed deep – oh so deep – into the earth. Hours later, each emerged with bulging eyes and a precious gem grasped tightly in its slobbery mouth. Then the swallows flew the uncut stones to an impoverished blacksmith, laid them in a circle on his workbench, and bade him do his finest work. (I understand they have promised to bring him more gems as payment). Just before dawn, these fine swallows picked up the necklace in their beaks and brought it to me. And now I am giving it to you.'

The princess barely heard the story, so entranced was she with the glitter and glimmer of the priceless stones. She gestured vaguely at the servant, turned and walked back towards the palace with the hunting dogs, the old woman forgotten. The old woman smiled to herself, prepared herself a light breakfast, then bundled her belongings into a neat backpack and continued on her way. Soon there was no sign that she'd been in the woods, except for the small ring of stones where she'd had her cooking fire. The red fox popped his head out of the underbrush, seized a small snack that the old woman had left for him, looked quizzically at the palace, then vanished into the woods. Before long all you could hear was the singing of the birds and the splash of a distant stream.

The princess' fascination with her diamond necklace lasted about a week. For eight days, she was gloriously content. Each day she would twist and turn in front of a mirror, admiring the silver galaxy around her neck. She attended balls just to show off her fine jewels, paraded through the town, and had her portrait painted while wearing the diamond necklace and not much else.

On the ninth day, however, she woke up feeling irritable. The diamonds suddenly seemed trashy, uncouth, somewhat commonplace. Surely another princess somewhere else had a finer set of stones. She turned to her long-suffering father with a petulant whine. 'Daddy, I want a palace made out of pink marble.'

Meanwhile, in a land far away from the princess, the old woman continued her journey, travelling with a light bag, a kind heart and an open mind. And the swallows, salamanders and fox continued to love, play and hunt in the woods, just as they have always done, just as they will always do.

Jealousy!

More time passes and I hear that the Sultan is away, quashing some bloody rebellion, far away to the north. They say that when he rides to hunt, or to make war, he rides the wildest horse that people have ever seen. She is a coal-black Arab mare, deep-chested and savage, unwilling to be tamed, unable to ever surrender. I imagine her charging into a swirling mêlée of armed men, bravely exposing her chest and underbelly, the Sultan's sword arm raised high. I know the exultation on his face at such a time, the need to constantly dominate or be dominated, his eternal lust for complete control. Over these thousand nights, I have come to know him so well.

It is a shock one evening, as I sit in front of my bedroom mirror, pinning up my hair, to see his face reflected in the glass. Still facing the mirror, I address his reflection. 'I have missed you,' I say simply, knowing it to be true, as unlikely as it may seem. He comes towards me, reaching strong arms around my shoulders and holds me tight. I smell sweat, dust, desert sand, a tired horse, smoke from a campfire, night air, stars, the male animal. I notice that his riding boots are stained with some dark liquid. Quickly his hands drop from my shoulders, and seemingly borne of an irresistible impulse, begin playing with my nipples through the fabric of my dress. He nuzzles his unshaven chin against my pale swan neck. Reaching both hands down so they cup the undersides of my breasts, he pushes them upwards, spinning me around so that he can pop first one erect nipple and then the other into his waiting mouth. 'And I you,' he eventually replies, an expression of lupine voraciousness splitting his lips into a broad grin.

'More than Olga?' I pout, instantly regretting the words. He pauses, carefully rearranges the bodice of my dress so that my breasts are once again covered, and slowly stands up.

'Who told you about Olga?' he asks, looking more perplexed than angry, his deep voice casual. I hang my head; if I give him the name, I am dead. He looks at me intensely, his eyes burning into the top of my skull. Then he is gone.

The Floating Village

The next morning, I wake with long, cool fingers of dread curled tight around my throat. I rise and walk around the room, coax my body to draw deep breaths, wipe damp palms against my thighs. At such times, I grab hold of my craft as a drowning sailor seizes a floating spar. The panic slowly subsides as I turn my mind to the evening ahead. Searching my memory for a story – a tale with enough force to charm my lover – I recall something that I heard in my village.

When I was a young girl, a desert trader came to our home. He rode into town on a flyblown donkey with all manners of things roped to its scrawny back: embroidery kits painted with black tulips; iron pots and pans; wicker cages full of tiny finches; bolts of shining blue China cloth; precious ivory fans. But the most valuable thing he carried with him was not for sale. On his final night in our village, after the town's housewives had purchased many of his items – at vastly inflated prices – he bought himself an excellent bottle of claret and sat down on a carpet in the middle of the town square. Smiling broadly at his assembled audience, he said, 'I would like to thank you for your hospitality by sharing a story.' The trader settled himself in the centre of the rug, poured himself a large glass of claret, and recited the following tale:

> There was once a village that ran out of salt. Now this may seem like a small thing – a matter of only trivial concern – but the discovery that there were no more hessian sacks full of these precious white crystals caused great consternation. The baker ran out of his shop howling, 'My bread is bland and tasteless!' The butcher stumbled drunk from the tavern sobbing, 'How will I preserve my meat?' And then everyone else in the village ran from their houses shouting, 'Our bread tastes terrible, and our meat is rotting as we speak. How will we live?'
>
> The village was in the worst country I have ever travelled. It was a strange place, located in the middle of huge sand dunes that behaved like humpbacked whales swimming across the earth. These dunes continually shifted, making maps impossible to draw. Riding along a ribbon-shaped road, one would look back, only to see mounds of sand moving towards each other, meeting and embracing like lovers. At night, wild storms rushed across the space and in the morning the landscape would be completely different.

The trader paused, sipped from a canteen of water, looking at us at thoughtfully with his bright eyes, seemingly miles away. He had a husky voice, the kind that soothes you in the same way as a swaying cobra mesmerises with its dance.

> I came across this village quite by accident, and was immediately set upon by the townspeople, who demanded to know if I had any salt to sell. Of course, being a well-provisioned desert traveller, I had a canvas sack of salt lashed to my donkey's back. I had never intended to sell the stuff, it was just to season my cook-

ing, but now I untied the bag and held it over my head. 'Who will buy my last bag of salt?' I cried.

The baker stepped forward, rubbing floury hands with glee. 'I will buy your salt for ten gold pieces.' The butcher shoved him to one side, 'I will have it for twenty!' he cried. And then a huge crowd of angry housewives mobbed me, some holding out handfuls of gold, a few baring their breasts, all desperate for my salt. The noise was terrible, with every single person in the village yelling at the top of their lungs, and in the background, the grinding noise of the giant sand dunes as they shifted to new positions.

Finally, when I thought the din could not get any louder, a young girl stepped forward. 'I will give you nothing for your salt,' she announced, 'and it is the best deal that you will ever make.' She grinned at me, supremely confident, and I could not help but smile back.

'How is this possible, child?' I asked, gesturing towards the handfuls of gold and the naked bosoms. 'Why should I not just sell my salt to the highest bidder? Or, perhaps, the loneliest widow?'

The little girl looked at me and sagely nodded her small head. She had large dark eyes and a grave expression. I found it impossible not to take her seriously, although I knew that what she was saying was ridiculous.

'If you sell the salt, your pockets will be heavy with gold. You will leave this village – if you can find your way through the sand dunes – and travel to a large city, where you will use some of the gold to drink and whore and eat fine food, and some of it to buy more goods to sell. Then you will resume your journey across the desert, with a freshly-stocked donkey, and once again sell your wares at inflated prices to isolated villagers.' I nodded, accepting the truth of what she proposed. 'And,'

she added, 'why would you take the widow instead of the gold, when you could sell your salt and have both?' Again, I nodded at the child's excellent common sense. 'Now imagine this instead,' said the little girl. 'What if you open that bag of salt and ask everyone to form a long line. As they pass, you will place a handful of salt in each palm, one by one, until the bag is completely empty. Then everyone will have enough salt to cook and preserve their food.' I looked at her blankly.

'You want me to give my salt away to the entire village, instead of selling it to one person?'

'Yes,' she replied calmly.

'And in what way do I benefit from such a trade?' I asked, beginning to get annoyed. The child looked at me with great patience.

'If you sell your salt to one man or woman, the rest of us will resent them. We will glare at this person with narrowed eyes and envy in our hearts.' I looked at the girl.

'Child, why is that my concern? Tomorrow, I will leave this village; you can sort it out amongst yourselves.'

The girl smiled gently. 'Of course, what you say is true. But imagine if you come back to our village in ten years' time. As a precious commodity acquired during a time of scarcity, the person who brought the salt would have risen to a position of high power and prestige, and those without access to salt will have long since become beggars.' I felt a little uncomfortable at this but had long since schooled my face to remain impassive during difficult negotiations.

'Again, my dear, why is this my concern?'

The girl looked at me as if I were a particularly dull student. 'At the moment, everyone can afford your wares. But when you return to the village, the rich will not be interested in the goods you have to sell, and the poor will not be able to afford them.'

I shrugged. 'Plenty more customers in other villages.' Nevertheless, she persisted.

'What will happen if you give your salt away?' said the girl with a grand flourish, clearly not expecting an answer. 'We will all be extremely grateful. The butcher will give you fine meat, and the baker will bring you fresh bread, and there is nothing better than a hot loaf just out of the oven. The housewives will be so relieved that they will ply you with excellent meals, and their husbands will buy you countless drinks. And the most desperate of the widows will welcome you into their beds tonight, and every night for a month. What more can you want, my friend?' I looked at the girl, and she looked at me, and I knew that I was beat. I untied my sack of salt, watched as the villagers formed a long line, and doled it out until my bag was quite empty.

The trader paused again and scratched his chin. 'What happened next?' asked one of the assembled villagers. 'Did you get the beer and the meals and the bread?' another said eagerly. There was a long silence as the trader looked around the circle of entranced faces.

'Yes,' he eventually replied. 'I got the tastiest cuts from the butcher, meat so soft it fell off the bone, juicy as spring rain. Bread that was only just out of the oven, soft and fluffy on the inside with a lightly salted golden crust. The housewives vied with each other to feed me their tastiest dishes, and their husbands brought me endless cold beverages, slapped me on the back and told me I was a good fellow.'

'And what about the widows?' asked one particularly cheeky brat.

'They were fine women, although exceptionally lonely,' smirked the trader, 'and I did not sleep for a month.'

The trader looked out past our faces, beyond the edge of the village and into the vast empty expanse beyond. 'After a month, I decided to go to the city to purchase more supplies – including a large supply of salt – and then return to this wonderful village…' He continued to gaze out into the darkness, and did not speak for a long, long time. I imagined that he was seeing a faraway country, a place where vast sand dunes undulate across the desert floor like migrating snakes, and small towns are swallowed up by limitless distances.

'Yes,' he finally sighed, 'if only I could find my way back there.'

> *The trader looked out past our faces, beyond the edge of the village and into the vast empty expanse beyond.*

Harem

But the next night it is as if nothing has happened. Again, the Sultan comes to my bedroom unannounced, this time bearing a gift. 'Close your eyes,' he orders. I feel him fasten something around my neck, and when I open my eyes, I run to the mirror and scream. A diamond necklace blazes against my throat, its radiance greater than a midnight galaxy. It is made of silver white stones linked by a fine gold chain. The jewels flash blue-white, glittering silver, pulsing and strobing like mirror fragments. I am overcome. I stand there, looking in the mirror, mesmerised by the perfection of the thing. This necklace makes me more beautiful than I thought possible.

He snuggles behind me, as affectionate as a kitten, and slyly asks, 'Were you really so jealous of Olga that it made you sick?' What could I tell him? How can I explain that while it may have been the trigger, the dark waters I swam in were far deeper than mere jealousy. Fear of a rival, even a beautiful dead woman, is nothing compared to the terror of losing oneself, of losing one's art. They are, I have come to realise, the same thing.

'Yes,' I answer, knowing that the lie will please him. He chuckles delightedly, failing to understand me, but valuing me even more in his error. If I were a child, he would have chucked me under the chin. Taking my shoulders, he spins me around and kisses me deeply on my mouth with such enthusiastic warmth that it astonishes me.

'Tonight, I have a special treat for you,' he says, taking my hand and leading me out of the door. Down, down, down the stairs we go, along a corridor I have never seen before, through two locked doors and briefly outside, passing through a marble courtyard full of date palms. I hear a monkey chatter in the treetops and a second later a ripe mango is hurled down, perilously close to our heads. Then we are inside again, climbing another flight of stairs and finally arrive in a nondescript dark hallway. He is still holding my hand as he turns, eyes glittering with excitement, one finger raised theatrically to his lips. We tiptoe along the hallway, both fighting an impulse to giggle. When the Sultan stops by a carved urn on the wall, I tug at his hand impatiently, eager to see my surprise, hoping for more jewels. He reaches up, clicks a tiny switch at the base of the urn, and a secret door swings open. I step back in shock. Bending double, he gestures at me to follow, so I duck my head and enter a tiny hidden room. Then he does something to the wall, and it snaps shut behind us with a firm click.

When my eyes adjust to the dark, I see that our secret chamber has black walls; it smells of recent paint and fresh incense. On the front wall is a decorative screen, and behind the screen is a brightly lit room with marble walls and exotic carpets that stain the floors with deep scarlet splashes of colour. It is so dark in here that the room's occupants will have no inkling of our presence. Without having to ask, I know that I am

looking at the Sultan's private harem. I see many gorgeous young courtesans, protected by dark-skinned male eunuchs, furnishings that bespeak the extremities of indolence and pleasure. In one corner of the room, I glimpse steam rising from a bathing pool, and a cold stream of water gushing down close beside. Like a garden of earthly delights, every person in this room is making love to another.

The screen in front of us is carved with animals and birds, the wooden beasts sometimes obscuring our view, so that we watch a man push his tongue into the carved breast of a robin, and a woman bending to suck the long curving head of an ornamental dandelion. I regard two men fondling the stem of delicate lily, as another passionately licks a stork's stripy leg. In every corner of the room, couples push and pull against each other in mutual submission and breathless ecstasy. I notice the pale blonde-haired maid with the unremarkable face, exposing vast peachy breasts. She kneels while behind her a black eunuch murmurs sweet things and rubs his fingers against her anus. Intrigued, I notice that she has a butterfly tattoo on her thigh, as blue as an old bruise, and that he has a carved wooden phallus strapped to his groin. The phallus and its straps have a raw, home-made look, as if assembled from found materials. I see the eunuch reach around behind him, his fingers searching for a little silver bowl; he draws it close and dabbles his fingers inside; when he withdraws them, they shine with oil. Then he alternates rubbing his large palms against her breasts – so huge that their nipples brush against the floor beneath her – and stroking her clitoris. I watch the woman's face redden, her body twitch with little shocks of ecstasy, his murmuring continue with the frequent

applications of oil to her breasts and cunt until her mouth drops open into a silent O. I see her lips taste the delight of a single word: 'Now.'

The eunuch tips the rest of the oil over his groin, the viscous liquid running down the phallus like syrup on a dessert, and he slowly pushes himself inside, stopping to ask her something, and when she nods, keeps moving until the whole length is buried between her plump buttocks. Sweat stands out on his brow and the woman is panting like a dog. In and out he pumps, controlling himself, savouring her climax, leaning forward, curving over her wet spine like a jockey, fondling the swollen nipples that brushed the floor with each stroke. The sight excites me so much that I am forced to look away.

My gaze turns to a couple embracing beside them. Two women stroke each other's long dark hair and take turns bending forward to lick nipples and nuzzle their partner's neck and face, a dance as ritualistic and exotic as courting swans. They too are talking, their conversation becoming shorter and more urgent as the caresses build to a climax. I watch their tongues intertwine, wander through the crevices of the other's mouth, searching for erotic sensation in the pristine skin of a neck. They are as entranced with each other, and as alike, as the vain princess in my book and her beloved mirror. At some point, by mutual agreement, one woman lies back and opens her legs like a book. 'Angela,' I hear her plead to her lover, who responds by lowering herself onto the floor, resting on her stomach, embeds her face into the other's body, with her forearms braced in a S shape against her partner's thighs.

Overcome by my desire, my mouth full of hot, fresh tasting saliva, I again look elsewhere. Beside me I hear the Sultan's breathing in hoarse gulps. Out of the corner of my eye, I see that he has removed his jacket and is seated beside me shirtless, his erect penis making a tent of the fabric between his legs. It is hot in this too small room, designed for the spying of one, not two. I remove my dress, leaving nothing but the diamond necklace, a lace corset, and a pair of high heels. I reach down and begin masturbating, still not looking at the Sultan, my little finger sometimes playing around the edge of my vagina, sometimes plunging deep when something I see excites me. Occasionally, I reach up to lick my finger, enjoying the warm musty taste, before letting my hands once again play between my legs. I push an embroidered cushion against the back wall of the room, bracing my feet against the wooden screen, allowing me to insert my fingers even further. After the briefest of pauses, I notice the Sultan has unbuttoned his trousers, freeing his hard cock, and is satisfying himself in long, slow strokes. Engaged in our private pleasures, we turn back to watch the figures in the room.

The eunuch has finished and is lying beside the blonde maid, his face propped on his hand, eyes intent on her face. She is smiling and sleepy, lying on her back, her full breasts falling down so that they disappear beneath her armpits. In a flash of sweetness, I notice that they are holding hands. Next to them the lesbians continue their passionate embrace, the girl on top fucking the other's cunt with her tongue, pausing to flick the tip against her lover's clitoris, and occasionally nuzzling so deep that her whole face seemed to vanish between her legs. The woman being so expertly tongued reclines, her fingers pinching the erect skin of her own nipples, now and again softening them with spit, and then resuming her steady caresses. Sometimes she lifts her head, viewing her lover's bobbing head with satisfaction, and pushes her own breast upwards so that she can tease the nipple with her long tongue. When this happens, I make three of my fingers into a triangular wedge and ram it deep into my wet pussy. Alas, my own breasts are too small to reach my mouth. No matter how hard I try, the nipples remained frustratingly out of reach. Watching me, the Sultan's hand strokes become more determined.

It is then that I glimpse something going on in a dark corner of the room, a trio of figures who I had previously overlooked. This is a moving sculpture of flesh, in a part of the room unlit by candles, and I can barely make out what I am seeing. As I stare, the picture gradually begins to make sense, and having recognised the truth of the scene, I push the triangle wedge of my fingers into myself with renewed vigour. Breaking off his own masturbation, I see the Sultan looking at me hungrily, his eyes shining in the darkness. Registering his intense concentration, I again lift my breast to my mouth and try to flick the erect nipple with my own tongue; an answering tongue darts out to moisten his lips.

Something in his urgent stare reminds me of my first night in the palace. After the green-eyed soldier abandoned me to my fate, and I had been given time to rest and bathe, I was presented to the Sultan wearing a simple cotton shift. By this time, I surmise, he had killed so many girls that his courtiers no longer bothered to adorn them, knowing that the soiled garments would have to be thrown away in the morning. Besides, servants are practical people, and what man ever noticed a gown? I stood before him, the latest virgin in a long line of victims, our flesh the living apology for another woman's sin. I felt sure that I would soon be dead.

But he was overcome. I stood there, thin from the fever, my small breasts clamped tight to my ribcage, nipples pushing against the white shift like drops of blood, my hair still short from my father's sword. The days of horseback riding had muscled my legs and browned my skin. I wore no cosmetics, nor jewellery, or anything else that would announce my gender. Crossing the room in fast strides, the Sultan yelled at his servants to get out; they fled the room, and he was on me, pushing me to the ground like a tiger pouncing on prey. I felt his stubbly chin grinding into my chest as he impatiently seized a mouthful of breast through the thin fabric of my shift. Plunging his hand between my legs, he impatiently forced my thighs apart.

Then he briefly sat back on his muscular haunches, eyes wild with desire, looking at me, drinking me in. It was the first and last time, since I came here, that he looked directly into my eyes. In a second, he was on me again, hands reaching out to rip open the neck of the shift, exposing my pointed breasts, his fingers grabbing the nipples like a greedy child seizes sweetmeats. Despite myself, my body began to stir, the frustration of sharing the green-eyed soldier's tent finally giving my body the voice it so urgently craved. I shook from my feet to the tip of my nose, great shudders thundering down my limbs, the open flower of my pelvis curled upwards, wet lips swollen scarlet. Desperately he ran his fingers through my short hair, again and again, unable to

seize a handful, his excitement mounting all the while. I felt him reaching towards a small table, his fingers snatching at a little vial of golden liquid, pulling it towards him and uncorking it in one swift movement. He flipped me over, urgently smeared olive oil between my buttocks and rammed his cock straight in.

At first the pain was excruciating, and I sank my fingernails deep into a pillow and howled like a dying dog. I screamed as he pumped and pummelled into me, a great rain of sweat falling from his brow, fists clenched around the bone basket of my pelvis, pulling me backwards and forwards at an ever-increasing speed. But he finished quickly. There was a giant cry of release, his body jerked like a spent animal, and I felt his penis pulse and jet inside me. Then he was done, exhausted, falling forward on top of me, asleep before we hit the ground, his stubble grinding into my shoulder blades, my buttocks bloody with semen.

Looking back, I think on that night he perceived me as a beautiful boy, a forbidden yet sanctioned vessel for his pleasure. In my country, no woman cuts her hair unless she is so infested with lice, or sick with fever, that no other course of action is tenable. Strange as it seems, my father's sword saved me from certain death that night. And having crossed one boundary, I think he decided to keep me alive to cross others.

The Wise Duck

I slumber for most of the following morning, occasionally waking to stretch my body against the cool weight of the bedding, then return to dreams. When I finally awake, I find that one of the servants has laid out a flowing dress embroidered with golden finches. With its sunset-coloured silk, and skirt that falls to the floor in diaphanous folds, the garment looks as if it is on fire. The little birds disappear into the crevices in the material, so that here and there you can see a tail vanishing into a shadow, or a sweet round head emerging from darkness. It looks as if they are flying in and out of an inferno.

During the night, the manservant has left a children's book sitting on the small table beside my bed. On the front cover is a picture of a black bird, sitting on a yellow straw nest, laying a blue-speckled egg. The egg is in the process of cracking open, and out of its hard shell scrambles another young bird, and on and on as far as the eye can see.

I flick open the book and begin to read:

> There was once a young girl whose father died, leaving her alone with a grieving mother, who sat alone for hours staring at their whitewashed cottage walls. The girl soon learned to cook and clean for them both and patched her dress when it grew thin. As the months passed, she watched as their meagre supply of coin grew smaller and smaller and finally disappeared altogether. Then the girl took their old cow to market,

and sold her for a few coins, and when that money ran out, she sold the goat, the sheep, and the hens, until all she had left was a single white duck.

The girl could not bear to sell the duck, who she had hatched from an egg, and often carried around the yard like a baby. The duck had a bright orange beak, snow-white feathers, and a fine pair of webbed flippers. One day, after the young girl and her mother had not eaten for three days, the duck turned to the girl and spoke. 'I think I know a way out of our predicament,' said the duck. The girl was too tired and hungry to ponder the impossibility of a talking duck.

'Great!' she said, 'What do you suggest?' And the duck leaned forward and whispered in the girl's ear. The girl's cheeks, which had been pinched blue-white with hunger, flushed rose-pink as she murmured, 'Ohhhh...'

The next morning Abigail – for that was the girl's name – rose early, tucked her duck under one arm, and set off for market. She tied a red spotted handkerchief over her hair and a matching cravat around the duck's neck. On the dusty road into the city, they were soon surrounded by the early morning traffic of farmers and merchants, all heading towards the market, all carrying heavy loads of fresh vegetables and fruit, pots and pans, bolts of cloth, household wares and the occasional luxury item, such as a mirror or vial of golden perfume. Abigail spied a rickety cart carrying a red wooden drum with a couple of jolly musicians on board. 'That's a fine-looking duck,' one of the musicians called out, as they trundled past. 'Are you taking it to market to sell?'

'No,' replied Abigail, 'this is a talking duck and I'm taking it to the city to meet the king.' The musicians laughed good-naturedly and wished her well.

When she arrived at the market, the girl set up a little stall at the edge of the animal tents with a hand-painted sign that proclaimed, '*Abigail and Her Fortune Telling Duck: Financial Guidance and Romantic Advice a Speciality*'. It was not long before she had her first curious customer. A portly merchant approached the stall, thumbs stuck into the pockets of his paisley waistcoat, and proceeded to inspect the duck. He was a rotund fellow in his later years with cheeks as blotchy as a vase of wilted roses, and a solid gold fob chain stretched across his ample belly. 'That is a good-looking duck,' observed the man, 'but no different to a million others. What makes you think it can talk?'

'If you would like a demonstration,' said the girl, 'you will need to pay one gold piece.' The merchant guffawed and flicked her a coin.

'Let's see it, then.'

Abigail grabbed the coin in mid-air, already thinking of the delicious food and nutritious seed she would buy herself and the duck. 'You have to ask it a question,' she said seriously. 'It doesn't just talk for fun.'

By this stage a decent crowd had gathered around the stall, with a keen array of onlookers, some waiting to see a rich man squander a gold piece for no good reason, and others hoping for the miraculous sight of a talking bird. The merchant stroked his chin and thought deeply. 'I am trying to decide whether to invest in my neighbour's cotton mill,' the man said. 'Simon tells me that I can double my initial investment of five hundred golden pieces within a year. My new wife thinks it is a good idea, as she loves pretty cottons and fine silks, but I'm still making up my mind. What would your duck advise?'

Abigail nodded sagely and put her head close to the duck's beak, listening intently. After a minute, she straightened up and looked at the man with a peculiar mix of pity and amazement. 'The duck says that neither your wife nor your neighbour is to be trusted, and that you would be a fool to invest in cotton. For a start, the duck thinks it will be a dry summer, so your neighbour's production costs will skyrocket. I'm sorry, sir,' and with this Abigail paused and looked closely at her duck, 'but it says that Simon and your wife are lovers. After the first five hundred gold pieces, Simon will come to you and ask for another two hundred, to buy machinery to harvest what he says will be a bumper crop. And after this two hundred, he will come to you for smaller instalments, and keep asking you for money until your fortune is gone. And when your gold has vanished, so will your young wife.'

'Gracious!' the merchant cried, clutching at his heart.

'I did not tell you this, but I have already given Simon five hundred gold pieces! And the rest is just as you have predicted: he came to me saying he needed new machinery, so I loaned him another two hundred. And yesterday he asked for another hundred, saying he needed to hire more pickers. But I did not give him the money, as something did not feel quite right, even though my wife urged me to do so.' The stricken man staggered away, roses completely drained from his cheeks. 'Tell your duck that that is the best gold piece I have ever spent!' he called before disappearing into the crowd.

'Next,' called Abigail, surveying the assembled bystanders. A lovesick young woman emerged from the throng and shoved her way to the front of the crowd.

'Ask your duck if Simon is the man for me!' she gasped, throwing down a coin.

By the end of the day, Abigail and her duck had amassed a large pile of golden coins. They ate and drank in luxury, then sent a basket of tasty food home for Abigail's mother. Early the next morning, they again set up their little stall at the edge of the market. It was not long before a troop of the king's soldiers arrived. 'The king would like to meet you and your talking duck,' their officer said, looking doubtfully at the ragged girl and her handkerchiefed duck. The officer escorted them to the palace, led them into the throne room, and left Abigail and her duck alone with the king.

The king was a very young man who liked reading history and writing poetry. He had only recently become monarch after his older brother – a muscular chap with polished armour and no ideas – died while out hunting wild boar. The king welcomed them warmly then looked curiously at Abigail and her duck. 'They tell me,' he said conversationally, 'that your duck appears to have a keen understanding of both financial markets and human behaviour. How is that so?'

'I don't know, sir,' admitted Abigail, 'he just started talking one day, when we were rather desperate. I think it's because he doesn't have any teeth or claws to protect himself. If you live in a world where you're potentially everybody's next meal, then I expect you have to become a pretty good judge of character. When I ask the duck how he knows stuff, he tells me that he looks at people's skin to see what they eat and drink, and he watches how they walk to see how they treat other people. He notices stuff that humans might not see.'

'I see,' said the king. 'That is indeed a useful attribute. Do you mind if I test it out?'

'Of course not, sir,' replied Abigail, smiling at her duck. 'We're happy to help.'

'Then I'll tell you what I want,' said the king, bending to speak conspiratorially in Abigail's ear.

That very evening, the king sat in his throne room with Abigail and her duck hidden by blue silk curtains behind his opulent chair. 'Are you ok back there?' he whispered. Abigail giggled and the duck let out a soft quack, which sounded more like a fart, sending the girl into peals of laughter. The king smiled, too, but fell silent as the doors to the throne room swung open and a large party of old men entered the room. These men were stately ambassadors from a neighbouring kingdom, whose king had long held designs on his neighbour's land, and they had come hoping to meet the muscular older brother. Instead, they were confronted by the sight of a bookish young man with round spectacles and a thin neck. 'Your majesty,' they said, bowing low and exchanging discreet glances under their eyebrows. 'We congratulate you on your coronation and come with many lucrative offers of trade and other mutually beneficial arrangements.'

With a dignified flourish, the most senior of the diplomats stepped forward. He was an elderly man with a long beard that almost swept the floor as he walked. 'Sire,' he said, bowing deeply, 'our king has ordered us to negotiate on his behalf. We would like access to your city's market to sell our wares. Our farmers are looking forward to a bumper crop of cotton this year, and it would be incredibly helpful if we could sell it here.

We will, of course, pay you a generous fee for this arrangement.' The king settled back in his chair, so that his head was closer to the blue silk curtain.

'Yes,' he drawled, 'a most interesting proposal. Excuse me for one moment while I consider it.' There was a hushed pause as the king, with his eyes closed, appeared to be murmuring to himself. The ambassadors looked at each other with consternation. Finally, the young king spoke.

'I have it from reliable sources that the cotton crop won't be quite the bumper harvest that some have anticipated. It seems to me that your farmers may have mistaken their market requirements.' The ambassador looked slightly irritated, but being a true diplomat, he hid it well. 'Then,' he continued, 'our king would like to extend an invitation to you to visit his country and meet his oldest daughter, the princess Sybil, who is as yet unmarried, and a very, er, fine young person.' Again, the king leant back in his chair and seemed to be lost in thought. Then he sat forward, bright eyes bulging slightly, and smiled at the ambassador.

'I am incredibly touched by your monarch's offer. I have one of my own. Unfortunately, I am too busy with the demands of public office to leave my country at this time, but I would love for the princess to visit my city. I promise to treat her with the utmost hospitality, and to introduce her to people with whom she may have an affinity.' Bowing and scraping, the negotiators withdrew, leaving the king alone with Abigail and her duck.

'Whew!' said Abigail. 'That was a lucky escape. Duck says that if you had let the foreign cotton farmers into the city market, they would have been soldiers in disguise, and you would have lost your kingdom and most probably your head.'

'Yes,' said the king, mopping his brow with a spotted handkerchief. 'Lucky indeed! And what does Duck have to say about the princess?'

'Duck says,' reported Abigail, 'that he heard from a flight of migrating ducks – it's a long flight and they like to talk – that Sybil is a nightmare on legs: spoiled, entitled and cruel. It would have been a miserable marriage, and if you had refused, you would have also lost your head.'

'Gracious,' said the king, 'Duck has certainly proved his value today. Why did you tell me to invite her here, then?' Abigail smiled slyly. 'To introduce her to Simon,' she replied.

From that day forward, Abigail, her mother and Duck all lived happily at the king's palace. The king was so pleased with their wise counsel that he changed his family's ancient coat of arms. Nowadays, if you travel to their kingdom, you can see the coat of arms proudly displayed on bright banners across the city and on many fine buildings. In one quadrant is a pair of yellow webbed feet, in the second a book, in the third a pair of round spectacles, and in the final square a red spotted handkerchief.

Secret

The following night we again creep to the harem, giggling like children as we hide ourselves in yet another secret room. Squashed into a tiny chamber, we find the room behind the screen brightly lit but empty. From our new vantage point, we can observe the bathing pool in its entirety, a steam room, and a large area of the floor padded with a white mattress. We fumble excitedly at each other's clothing and exchange frenzied kisses, waiting for the show to start. I press my belly up against the carved panel and the Sultan grasps me tightly from behind, whispering in my ear and laughing, his fingers working away at my clitoris, teasing me into febrile delight.

The first person to enter the room is the blonde maid with the unremarkable face, a short dress revealing her thigh with its butterfly tattoo. She stretches and calls out to someone over her shoulder. Expecting to see her previous lover, I am surprised when she is joined by another woman: a blonde courtesan from the harem. A gorgeous young woman, the courtesan is long legged and slim, with an elegant profile. The two women wander over to the padded floor, the maid talking animatedly, occasionally circling the courtesan, who appears bored with the whole encounter. I watch the maid run one finger up the inside of the courtesan's arm, gently tug her blonde hair, then lightly reach forward to brush both her palms against the other woman's nipples, talking quietly the whole time. She circles the courtesan again,

coming closer this time to push aside her mane of blonde hair and nip the back of her neck; now a shudder runs through the girl's body. Swiftly the maid resumes her position in front of the girl, dipping her hands into the other's gown and caressing her breasts. Leaning forward she pushes the breast into her elastic mouth and gorges on it, sucking and kneading gently with her fingertips, sometimes breaking off to murmur some more, using her spare hand to lightly flicker against the other nipple. When the courtesan begins to murmur and sway slightly on her feet, the maid changes tack. She suddenly kneels, pushes up the girl's gown and plunges her tongue between her legs. The courtesan cries out and leans forward, bracing her hands against the maid's back, her face bouncing up and down with her vigorous licking. They tumble down onto the mat, the maid tugging her clothes off and then removing her own, lying on top of the girl with her mouth on the courtesan's breasts and one hand clamped between her legs.

From my vantage point, I can see the courtesan's face turned towards me, her red lips parted with pleasure, a little trail of spit oozing from the side of her mouth. She moans and bites her lips, and as the maid continues to penetrate her with avid fingers and suck at her breasts, the courtesan's body arches with wave after wave of ecstasy. Then just as quickly as before, the maid sits back and spins her body so that her face is buried in the courtesan's sex, offering her own genitals to the other's eager tongue. Lounging with thighs locked

around each other's heads, rolling, sucking and tonguing, their bodies writhe just in front of our screen, the sight of which causes my body to tremor with orgasm. The pleasure mounts to the point where it degenerates into exquisite pain; on the verge of screaming out, I slap the Sultan's hand aside and drag my gaze away from the two blondes.

> # The pleasure mounts to the point where it degenerates into exquisite pain; on the verge of screaming out, I slap the Sultan's hand aside and drag my gaze away from the two blondes.

By the side of the bathing pool kneels another courtesan, her ebony skin beaded with sweat, her muscled body quivering in the staccato beats of sexual congress. Her head lowered, I realise that she is carefully bouncing a man's mouth up and down against her genitals. He stands in the pool, chest splashing against the surface of the water as she cradles him between her legs. Meanwhile another man fucks her from behind with steady, rhythmic strokes, the penetration forceful yet smooth. Tipping her forwards, while holding her firmly by the hips, the man uses a leather phallus, tightly bound around his hips, to bounce her against his groin. I soon realise that he is carefully timing his thrusts to co-ordinate with those of the man below. Drawn by the trio's intense pleasure, the two blondes disentangle themselves and slip into the water, graceful as cats, either side of the licking man. Ducking their blonde heads, they take turns sucking on her breasts and reach wet hands up to stroke her clitoris.

Watching this group, I feel my mouth fill up with hot liquid and my cunt swell in anticipation. I push my lover up against the wooden screen and grab his penis, urgently rubbing him with my slippery palms. He arches his back, silently moaning with pleasure, forehead streaming with sweat. Before he has a chance to object, I climb up onto the screen, holding on with simian fingers and toes, and push the full length of his penis into my vagina. I slam myself against him with great hard strokes, riding his longed-for organ for the first time, a cry of exultation boiling up within me. Just as quickly, I am hurled down onto the floor, the Sultan stands over me, shaking with anger, his penis wet with my juice. Looking down at me, he takes himself to orgasm with quick, deft strokes. An explosion of semen rains down on me, as warm as summer rain.

The Three Rules of Dying

I do not sleep that night, but neither am I fully awake, poised between epiphany and despair, teetering on the feverish edge of reason. Terror nests on my chest like a contented cat. It seems at one point that my mother comes to me, smooths a cool palm across my burning forehead, but when I open my eyes, it is the manservant who I see slipping away. The white ceiling of the room undulates in waves, and there is nothing I want more in this world than to be back in my village, sleeping in my childhood bed, with my family close beside.

Again and again, I imagine the door bursting open, soldiers carrying sharpened blades, then a red stain spreading across my bed. Or worse, killers who move with the silent grace of hunting tigers, cutting me to pieces as I slumber. For some reason, I dread a sleeping death more than a waking one. If one must die, it is best to do so standing on one's feet, with eyes wide open, and full knowledge of what is about to transpire; there is something awful about slipping from one oblivion to another. An ancient rule, only learned by the dying, that one must greet death like the best and oldest of friends.

A lock of hair tickles my forehead. Reaching up, I am perturbed to feel feathers brush against my fingertips. A hummingbird is sitting on my bedhead, looking down at me with its bright little eyes. It has twined my hair into a rough nest, lined it with soft feathers, yet when it opens its beak, my mother's voice comes out. 'Your time here is nearly over,' it says, preening at its wing feathers with its sweet scimitar of a beak. 'You've learned your craft well,' notes the bird, looking at me with approval.

'Yes,' I agree, propping myself up on one elbow. Over these thousand nights, in the searing press between sunset and dawn, I have told many stories with words and skin.

I notice that the manservant has left some sweet delicacies on the small table beside the bed, so I pop a honeyed fig into my mouth. The juices explode in a ripe constellation of popping seeds, and so I discover the second rule of dying: if one must depart, it is better to do so on a full stomach. I swallow a delicious mouthful of sugary goo and lie back on the bed.

The hummingbird gives me a stern look, snaps one final feather into place. 'If you're ever going to be an artist,' it says, 'you'd better do it now.' And with that it rises, hovering in mid-air above my head, jewelled wings fanning cool air against my face, and flies towards the window. At the last moment, it turns its head sideways and glares at me with one magnificent blue eye. 'Art is long and life is short,' it quips, flying up and away into the velvety black sky.

For hours after the hummingbird's departure, I lie there pondering its words. My body hums with fever and my mind will not rest. I picture everything I could do in my life, and although I am still young, count the multitude of gifts I have already squandered. And then, as the stars flicker out and the night sky fades into yet another anodyne day, I stumble on the third and most bitter rule of dying.

There is never enough time.

Day

The following day arrives overcast and bleak. I remain in bed, waiting for something, I know not what. But when the Grand Vizier steps out of the shadows, I am not surprised; somehow I knew the Sultan would lack the courage to kill me himself. The Grand Vizier seems to have shrunk since our last meeting, a certain frailty has crept into his steps, though he is still deadly as nightshade. His hands shake and once during our conversation, he turns away to cough, a dry rasping sound, like bones grating on dead sand. I sense the desperation lurking beneath his malevolence. I should know it when I see it: these thousand nights anxiety has haunted the corridors of my mind. It has stalked me like a hungry wolf during a long famine. Fear has been as constant as my shadow.

He starts by threatening me, that old chestnut, telling me more stories of outlandishly beautiful dead women. And when jealousy or self-doubt fails to flare, he resorts to more direct methods. He cries out that I will be dead soon, that the Sultan is tiring of me, I am growing old, fading, and will soon be meat for the beasts. I listen impassively, waiting for him to come to the point, wondering at the evil that lives within men, within all men. I let his words flow over me, impervious to their poison, watching as he tires himself. Exhausted by his tirade, the old man turns away to cough. I listened to the bones of his throat squeezing together, the sound of a cracked leather accordion with a hole in the bellows, a grainy rasp of imprisoned phlegm. *You, I think, will be dead sooner than I.*

Then he passes me a package, and I unwrap it. It is more money than I have ever seen. At midnight, the Grand Vizier says, my door will be left unlocked, and also the door at the bottom of the staircase, with a waiting bag of clothes, then safe escort to the palace gates. Once the gates have swung shut behind me, I will find a horse and rider, waiting to take me wherever I wanted to go. I look at him and know he lies, without compunction, with no honour. If there is a rider waiting for me, he will be harbouring a long blade, blackened with grease so it does not shine in the moonlight. My bones would be scattered across the desert floor before dawn, dark flowers of blood all that remain of my body. I hand the package back. 'You will regret it!' he screams, his face terrible, beyond ancient, the evil of the depths surging upwards, flooding across the haggard human skin. I shrug and hold his gaze. Unaccustomed to such defiance, he trembles with fury and leaves. I am certain that he will not rest until I am out of the Sultan's bed.

Morning passes. The manservant brings me my breakfast and then retires to let me eat. I watch rain clouds form over the perennially blue sky and feel the faint stirrings of a southerly breeze whisper through my window. I am not surprised when I hear the door creak open behind me and sense a woman standing close. When she places her hand on my shoulder, I turn to find a blonde woman, the maid with the unremarkable face, looking straight into my eyes. It is curious, but having watched this woman with her lovers, I feel a strange affection for her, and am sad to discover that she is one of the Vizier's creatures.

Yet her approach is infinitely subtler than his, and for all their charms, that much the deadlier. She begins by searching my eyes with her own, then talking about how she misses her village; loving aristocratic parents; her kidnap by the Sultan's soldiers; incarceration as a servant, followed by mistreatment and loneliness. She grabs my hand, squeezes out a tear and lowers her head. A plump tear splashes on my skin, and her agile fingers begin to stroke the underside of my palm. She comes closer, but I am wise, having seen the same trick played on the young courtesan. She makes to collapse in a fit of sobbing, attempts to throw her arms around my neck, pleading kinship and loyalty. I wait to see what she will do next. When she reaches forward to brush her palms against my nipples, I stand up, telling her to stop.

Fear of disappointing the Grand Vizier twists her face into awful patterns, I think of an animal caught in a trap, the grimace of pain as it struggles to be free. She pleads that she loves me, she needs to be close to me, was I so heartless as to dismiss her friendship? I remain impassive. Urgently she tugs down the front of her dress, an enormous peachy breast spilling out. 'I will give this to you,' she says, raising the nipple to her own mouth and sucking like a spoiled child, 'you can do what you want to me.' When I turn away, she runs at me, catching my shoulders and spinning me around. 'Wait!' she cries, then bending down opens a cupboard near the window, a non-descript piece of furniture I had never noticed before. She drags out a strange slab of timber

with the four legs of a stool, the top adorned by two enormous carved malachite horns, the whole object sporting the profile of a bull's head.

'If it is cock you want,' she hisses, 'try this.' Raising her skirt, and exposing her shaved blonde pubis, she drops herself down onto the stool, impaling herself on a malachite horn, grunting with the effort. 'You sit facing me,' she orders, laughing with nervous animation, 'and I will suck your breasts as we bounce upon these fine horns.' I laugh, I cannot help myself, for the sight of an unaroused woman bouncing on a cold green spike, talking about all the things she will do to me, has a certain kind of tragic comedy.

'Fuck off,' I tell her, the gutter language of my village returning to my mouth as naturally as the air that I still breathe. 'And take your stinking fucking excuse for a stool with you.' She leaves, head down, suddenly tired. I guess she knew that she was dead.

The Little Mermaid

Deep under the sea, in the heart of the ocean, there is a splendid castle made of pink seashells and bone-white coral. The place is surrounded by a dense forest of dark green kelp and is almost hidden from view. And although few people – other than drowned sailors – have ever seen the palace, it has been there for hundreds of years, perhaps thousands. For on the bottom of the sea floor, time passes even slower than in the desert.

In the palace lived the last of the Sea King's daughters, a robust young woman with a wave of sea-green hair and a body crusted with silver oysters. Her neck flared with the lace of magnificent gills, and her whale tail was lined with sinewy muscle. When the mermaid swan through the ocean, sharks would dart away like scared goldfish, whales turned politely aside, and even the giant squid – normally a cantankerous soul – would remember his manners and let her pass. In the darkness of the deep ocean, the mermaid was perfectly content.

One day, on the first day of spring, the mermaid decided to visit the surface of the ocean. It had been a long time since she had seen a sunset, and as few things on the ocean floor are pink or orange, she missed the sight of these vibrant colours. She swam up through layers of water that were coldly blackish blue, traversed a slice of midnight blue sea, ascended through dark green, indigo and turquoise waters, and finally popped her head out through a delicious froth of aquamarine bubbles. Right in front of the mermaid, silhouetted against the setting sun, was a three masted sailing ship.

The ship was lying on its side like a dying turtle. Sailors scurried across the hull, attempting to right the vessel, cutting away sails that were dragging the boat down into the sea, but to no avail. It was clear to the mermaid, and to the sailors too, that the ship would soon settle on the bottom of the ocean with a fresh crew of drowned men. On the bow, outlined in gold leaf, was carved the ship's name, The Nematode.

Now the mermaid, like most sea creatures, had long since turned away from the lives of those who make their home on land. She was not cruel – far from it – it was simply that once you have seen the bottom of the ocean, and the setting sun glowing far above, most other concerns seem minor in comparison. But on this particular evening, driven more by curiosity than anything else, she swam alongside the stricken vessel and peered in through a submerged porthole.

Through the circle of timber, she saw a young man floating in a luxurious cabin. Swathes of silk curtain and golden goblets and many other fine things were suspended in the water around him. His mouth was open in a perfect O, and she saw that his skin would soon be cold and blue. On an impulse, the mermaid smashed the porthole glass with her strong tail, dragged the young man out of his cabin, through the tangle of rigging and stays, and up onto the surface of the sea. As the sun dipped below the horizon, flooding the sky like a bouquet of fuchsias, roses and marigolds, the stricken vessel disappeared beneath the waves. The mermaid pressed her gills against the young man's mouth and gave him the gift of life.

Holding the unconscious man tightly in her arms, she swam towards land and dragged him up onto a deserted beach. All through the night she wrapped her body around his, keeping his human skin warm, and in the first light of dawn she slipped back into the cold blue sea. The young man opened his eyes, saw nothing but white sand, salt-water and a merciless sky, but remembered – as if in a dream – the touch of the mermaid's hands and the smooth feel of her gills against his parted lips. He sat up, astonished, looking for his saviour, but the mermaid ducked her head beneath the waves and swam back to her home on the ocean floor.

Years passed like minutes on the sea floor. On dry land, the young man was crowned king after his elderly father died. Time flowed like a spring tide, relentlessly washing away all in its path. As the kelp around the mermaid's palace swayed like dancing girls, the young man watched his children born, grow, fall in love, and have children of their own. One morning, when he looked in the mirror, a wrinkled, grey-haired man stared back at him. While he was perfectly comfortable in his life – wearing it like a leather coat that has softened with age – and although his family and people had prospered, the mermaid's act of grace niggled at him like a stone in his shoe. As his life force slowly waned, he could not forget his unpaid debt.

The following year, on the first day of spring, the king sailed out of his harbour in a three masted sailing ship. The captain steered the boat to the place where the young man had almost drowned, all those years ago, and then they furled the sails and sat there bobbing on the glassy sea. The king ordered the sailors to take turns beating on wooden drums, and the sound of the instruments reverberated through the hull, deep down into the water, until it finally reached the ocean floor. The mermaid watched the kelp shaking in tiny, rhythmic shudders and then, with a giant flick of her powerful tail, launched herself toward the surface to investigate.

It was sunset when she finally poked her head out through the silky surface of the sea. Overhead, giant flowers of crimson, magenta and lemon-yellow light blazed across the sky. The three masted ship sat there, sails neatly strapped to its yard arms, and alone on deck was the solitary figure of a very old man. The mermaid swam through the sea to the boat, hauled herself up over the rail and onto the deck. The old king and the mermaid looked into each other's eyes, one a creature from the bottom of the ocean with a palace ringed by swaying kelp forests, the other with a stone palace surrounded by straight trees in a land of sand, dirt and rock. And in that moment, they knew one another, and were at peace.

Spurt

I do not see the Sultan that night, nor the next, or the next. There is a feeling afoot that something has changed in the palace, some important news about to break; a general sense of charged anticipation. Servants move quickly, looking worried and tense, dropping objects. I hear footsteps running along the corridor outside my bedroom at night. Outside the weather turns slowly hellish; I sit by my window and watch storm clouds roll like ocean waves, the awful green light of a mounting southerly gale. In their golden cage, my finches become timid, flitting from one perch to another; in their minds they think they are outrunning the storm. I wait. We all wait. Throughout the city I sense men and women looking at each other with concern, glancing up at the sky, praying with renewed fervour. In the animal tents at the market, fewer lies are told than is usual. As the sky turns grey, the night arrives in the early afternoon, a ghostly premature twilight that sucks all the colour from the world. The palace carpenter arrives to repair a broken shutter, which slams ominously against my window. 'I have never seen a sky like this,' he mutters, elderly face creased with concern.

That evening, when the wind drops without warning, and the palace swelters in the sudden heat and blackness, the Sultan sends for me. A squadron of maids arrive with instructions to dress my hair up in tortoiseshell combs and adorn me in a blue silk dress, shining China cloth, the colour of a summer sky. They flit around me, pinning things and powdering, even using tiny combs to arrange my eyelashes. Eventually they finish, and I stand there, as close to a living doll as it is possible to be; I thank them and send them from the room. Then only the manservant is hovering, waiting to usher me to the Sultan's bedchamber. We listen as the maids' twitter fades down the corridor, a group of noisy girls nervous and awed by the coming storm; we stand there alone, looking at each other. Unceremoniously, I pull the silk dress over my head and dump it on the floor. I throw my head back, drag the tortoiseshell combs out of my thick hair, and drop them on the dressing table. Finally, I grab a cloth and wipe the carefully applied powder from my face. When I have finished, the only thing I wear is the Sultan's priceless diamond necklace.

As the manservant rushes around like an anxious hen, I push open the door to my room, and calmly walk naked down the corridor outside, little flickers of lightning illuminating my pale flesh. The corridor is black in the unnatural night, but as I walk past the arched windows, lightning blazes and flashes against my skin. Beside himself, the manservant wrings his hands and beseeches me to put on a gown, a wrap, something, anything! I ignore him, merely wait for him to unlock the necessary doors, enjoy the power of moving through the world without clothes, the electricity in the air curling the tiny hairs on my arms and legs. Each thunderclap sends answering shivers of excitement through my body. Unable to extinguish my nudity, the manservant gives up and retreats, I hear his worried quacking recede as he flees down a

corridor. I come to the door I have visited a thousand times before. When I knock on his door, the Sultan opens it himself.

We stand there, looking at each other, the woman who wasn't meant to live and the man who wasn't meant to love. I put my hand on his chest and push past him, entering his domain, liking the sensation of my damp thighs stroking against each other. I sashay over to the bed, letting my hips undulate in small circles, my spine a velvet ribbon. A bolt of lightning lights up the room so that it burns like daylight. And then he is on me, covering the distance from the door to the bed in a few steps, panting with desire, using his strong arms to pin me down, down onto his bed. My body bucks as if struck by lightning. I marvel at his ravenous mouth devouring my breasts, tongue racing down my body to explore every part of my sex, his penis leaving a trail of fresh seed against my thigh. I want him as I have never wanted anything before.

There is a loud crash overhead, it sounds like the storm is directly overhead or that lightning has struck the building. As his body writhes and his mouth sucks, I behold the dreadful power of a once-in-a-century storm, unleashing its wrath on the thin roof over our heads. I cling tight to my lover, wrapping my legs around his thrusting pelvis, as he ravages my breasts with his tongue. Then suddenly the rain arrives, falling out of the sky in a solid block of water, beating on the palace roof like a thousand hammers, impossible to hear, impossible to speak, impossible to think.

I push him off me and shove him onto his back. The noise is so deafening that the world is plunged into a peculiar silence: I cannot hear my own movements or feel my own heartbeat. In a world of chaotic noise and darkness, senses grow in new ways. Out of the darkness, I feel his eyes looking directly into my face, and I know he is seeing me for the first time. A wise woman once told me that freedom is never given– it must be taken. As he looks into my eyes, and I his, I feel a boundary crossing as profound as it is wordless. Some people would call it love but I know now that this word is never wild enough.

Pushing a pillow under his hips to increase my pleasure, I climbed on top of him, and lower my soaking cunt onto his hard organ. Bouncing until my flying breasts are jagged with pain, my clitoris sore and swollen as if it will explode, I ride him like an unbroken horse. One hand clamped between my legs, toying with my clitoris, the other cupping my breast and rubbing the nipple to an agonising point. All around us the wall of water drenches us in white noise; no matter how hard I slam his body into the mattress, there is no sound. I can tell he is screaming with pleasure, but although his mouth is wide open, a cavernous black O in the darkness, I can hear nothing. In that moment, in that void of sensuality and noiselessness, my mind and body meet and become one. When I come, liquid gushes out of me in a geyser, pools of water drenching his cock, pouring off his body onto the sheets, spreading like a giant fountain across the bed. Water everywhere, thrown from my body onto the sheets (this has never happened before!) rushing from the palace roof in sudden waterfalls, overcoming spouts and guttering, an invading army of unstoppable force. On the damp bed, we cling to each other, mute survivors of a shipwreck.

Inland Sea

That night I dream that I am back in my parents' house. My father stands by the fireplace, stroking his unshaven chin, sword in hand. Somewhere out in the vast expanse of the golden desert, the Sultan's soldiers are coming for me. In the dream, I can see the smoke from their campfire spiralling upwards like a genie, their horses a deadly arrow pointing straight at the heart of my village.

My father's hands tremble as he hacks at my raven hair with his sword. Down it falls, down into great clumps on the stone floor, lying soft and silky as dead ravens. Meanwhile my mother sweeps it into the fire, tears trickling down her face, the drops splashing like spring rain on the dry stone. Her tears land on the ragged chunks of hair and sparkle like dew.

As my scalp emerges, blue-white and dusty through the remaining tufts of hair, a strange kind of magic takes hold. My hair begins to grow, slowly at first, then quicker and quicker, faster even than my father's sword can cut it away. It grows thicker than before, dark with the oily blackness of tar, coarse as a mare's mane, strong as spider silk. My parents back away as hair springs from my head, snaking through the house, knocking plates off the table and a wooden goblet from the shelf.

Soon it pushes open the door, out into the garden, then beyond this, coiling and springing, running in all directions like water dropped from above.

It multiplies as it grows, curling sensuously strong around tree trunks, dipping its furry ends into dry wells, gripping hold of passing sheep and goats, pushing onwards across the desert like a giant black lake. Unstoppable, it twists itself around mountains, fills valleys in an instant, travels beyond the reaches of the desert and finally arrives at the sea itself.

When it reaches the sea, it pauses briefly, then dives in, flowing with the absolute grace of an enormous octopus, with a million arms swirling and preening in all directions. Before long, there is nothing left but hair: ships sail through its waves; whales dive into its silken depths; eels twist themselves around strands, tying themselves into knots tighter than vengeance. In this parched land of sand and dust, I wake with the taste of the ocean in my mouth, and my mother's voice insistent, ringing like a great bronze ship's bell in my head. I know, without thinking about it, that I am going home.

I know, without thinking about it, that I am going home.

End

There are no more stories; there are no more nights. I wake in the Sultan's bed, with him in it, and lie there listening to the storm recede. At some time during the darkness, infinite sadness sweeps over me, a grief for something that has never been, and now is gone. I tell no stories, but cry until my tears soak the feather pillow. It stinks of wet duck. All night the Sultan's arms are around me, his soft penis curled obligingly into the small of my back, curved like the spiral end of a fern.

In the morning, he walks me back to my room; we bump against each other and kiss, just ordinary lovers, his hand clutching mine. Endings are all around us, even the stone walls seem sad. I press my body against his to try and keep out the cold, the melancholy that waits only a heartbeat away. At this moment, we cannot bear to be parted, so he comes into my room with me, putting it off as long as possible. While I dress, he wanders over to pull the night cover off the birdcage. The heavy fabric falls off in a rush, revealing the lustrous golden bars and a hundred tiny birds, living beings infinitely more wonderful than any metal. I watch as he opens the birdcage hatch, and a waterfall of finches spills out of the cage. They circle the room, hundreds of luminous wings beating around my face, and then they are gone, out the window and up into the waterlogged sky. 'Some of them,' remarks the Sultan drily, 'will be eaten by sunset.' But then he takes my hand and kisses me before leaving, adding an apology: 'I have some things that I need to take care of.'

I sleep the dreamless slumber of a loved child. When I awake, the manservant is standing there, looking grave and rather drained. 'My master suggested you may like a walk in the menagerie,' he courteously offers, holding out a warm cloak. It is clearly not an invitation that can decently be refused, so I allow him to help me into the cloak. The warm red wool holds the cold at bay, an icy emotion that chills my blood and threatens to invade my bones. I had never realised that leaving a cage could hurt so much.

We walk out into the palace gardens. This time the manservant does not bother to blindfold me, as if he knows that I will never come this way again. We stroll through gardens so magnificent that my breath catches in my throat; I walk into a marble courtyard with a long pool and carp the size of dogs, waterlilies as big as my head are buffeted by muscular fish tails. We pass a solitary nightingale singing on a lemon tree, crying with the passion of an opera singer, its voice more human than bird. I wonder why this bird is awake during the day, decide that the storm must have unsettled its mind. The manservant leads me through a meadow of wildflowers, a beautiful impossibility in this country of dust and stone. Soon we arrive at the huge iron gates of the menagerie, the gates that separate man from beast, but in my heart, I know that such a division does not exist.

After the beauty of the gardens, I am not in the mood to watch stinking predators vilify the bars of their cages, yet my lover has sent me here with his most trusted servant, perhaps even his friend, and I know that I must remain. 'They will start feeding them soon,' murmurs the manservant, taking my elbow and guiding me out of the way of a man pushing a large wheelbarrow full of fresh meat. I step back, the smell repulsing me, and now the wild animals scent it too, battering themselves against the metal bars. Leopards bark their snarling cough, the lions bay with blood-hungry thunder and the jackals excitedly yip-yip-yip their murderous chant. All around us, claws twist around metals, tails thrash and glowing eyes sharpen with savage rage.

The man pushing the wheelbarrow is wearing the leather apron and sturdy gloves of his trade. I notice the large loops of his knife belt and that his shoes are soaking wet. Staggering towards the animal cages with an armful of meat, he turns slightly towards me, deliberately pausing so I can view the severed head on top of the pile. Despite the many bruises, something about the head's long white beard, straight as a spear, looks very familiar. I turn away, recognition forcing a spurt of vomit up into my mouth, for I do not have a vengeful soul, and I would not wish such an ending on anyone, even the Grand Vizier. Overhead the sky is grey and below the mud bloody and wet. As we turn to walk back towards the palace, I am almost sure that I see the man feeding a human thigh, spotted with the delicate bruise of a butterfly tattoo, to a choking leopard.

I am still pale with shock when we reach my room. The manservant sets lunch on the table, and seeing my appalled glance at the cold meat he has placed in front of me, silently clears his offer-ings. I sit there staring at my empty birdcage, the room devoid of light and life since the tiny birds fled. I sense that the manservant wants to tell me something but struggles to find the words. 'What happened?' I ask him, looking straight into his black eyes. The manservant blushes but deter-minedly holds my gaze.

'I told him what happened,' he says simply, 'I waited outside the Sultan's bedroom door when the Grand Vizier visited you for the first time. I waited again when he came yesterday, and when he sent the blonde maid to seduce you.' It is strange. I have known him for many moons now, but until today I never realised that he has grown up, changed from boy to man. It is as odd as seeing a little child with wrinkles and a grey beard. In a flat voice he went on, 'If the maid had succeeded, she would have led you to the harem, at a time she knew the Sultan was waiting behind the secret screen. He would have watched you with other men and women, and he would have enjoyed it, but in the morning he would have killed you.'

I give a little jump. I had thought our secret visits to the harem had passed unnoticed. 'No,' says the manservant, 'they knew you were there.' Looking tired, he moves towards the door, carrying my silver luncheon tray with its untouched food. 'It was all art,' he says, and with that he is gone.

Freedom

That night we are slow with each other, riding waves of ecstasy in unison, until the sounds of a cock crowing bursts the night silence, and the square of the window fades to a dark ultramarine. I lie in his arms watching the stars flame and flicker, my body drenched with sweat, all desire gone. This is my last night in this place, I know it as clearly as if he has told me so. For some reason, he has decided to let me go, or rather he has decided not to stop me leaving. Before the last star has faded from the sky, I arise from our comfortable embrace, kiss him lightly on the lips (I know he feigns sleep) and whisper my eternal gratitude into his ear. A spasm ruptures the lids of his closed eyes and I know he struggles not to reach out and grab me, to control what he can never tame. Although the man lying on the bed in front of me is a murderous beast, I feel a kinship with him that I will never find with another. He is the nightmare that made me human.

But now it is time to go. I tiptoe from the Sultan's bedchamber and I do not turn back. I know that decisions are made on the edge of a heartbeat, and that if I do not leave quickly, I never will. The lock slides open and as quiet as a cat, I return to my room, hastily stuff a few clothes and some food into a pillowcase. I have my hand on the doorknob when I freeze. Walking across the room for the last time, I open my dresser and pull out the box with the diamond necklace. I leave, slipping this circle of stars around my neck.

I descend the stairs, through the heavy wooden door which has mysteriously been left unlocked, through another door and there I see a leather bag sitting on the ground. Picking it up, I find a knife, bag of money, water canister, food, riding boots and a warm cloak. I smile to myself as I hoist the bag over my shoulder, push open the final door and walk through the dark gardens, heading towards the palace gate. Slipping between shadows, I near the gates, heart beating furiously when I see an armed guard patrolling their length, the deadly question mark of a scimitar hanging from his belt. He is an older man with blonde hair, a soldier's face hardened by bloodshed, and large hands made for killing. Coming closer, I notice that the gates have been left slightly ajar, a gap big enough for one person to slip through, no more. Waiting until the guard's back is turned, I pass silently through the gates. I may be imagining things, but I think he averts his gaze, pretending not to see me.

Then I am outside the city walls, the palace rapidly receding as I hurry down the desert road, wanting to get as far away as I can before sunrise. When the sun comes up, I will be as visible as a fly on a white tablecloth. I have taken a hundred steps, no more, when I hear hoofbeats approaching fast behind me. My spirits, which have risen high upon traversing the iron curtain of the palace gates, plunge deep into the dust to be crushed underfoot. After so many nights, I will be captured at the moment of my escape, dragged back to a life with no future. I gasp with the pain of disappointed hope.

The rider pulls his horse up in front of me. I stand there sullenly looking at his foot in the metal stirrup. A familiar voice asks from above, 'May I be of any assistance?' Looking up, I recognise the manservant grinning from the back of an Arab mare, a horse bred with strong legs for speed and a deep chest for stamina. Such a horse can carry you across a desert in a single night. He dismounts, long legs dropping onto the ground beside me, a smile breaking across his face at my surprised expression. 'How did you know?' I stammer, pointing back towards the palace gates, and holding up my leather bag with a shrug.

Outside the palace walls, holding the reins of this fine mare, the manservant is a different creature: proud and self-assured. I look at his dark eyes and his straight back, his broad chest just starting to fill out, and suddenly he seems familiar, achingly so. 'It is my job to know,' he proudly replies. 'The Sultan relies on me to be his eyes and ears, to tell him what the other courtiers dare not.' Handing me the reins, he deftly straps my leather bag onto the back of the saddle, quickly gives me directions and tells me where I can stop for food and shelter. I listen to him, feeling numb, amazed to discover an ally in such an unlikely place.

'Why don't you come with me?' I ask him. 'If you go back there, one day you will displease him, and then you'll be food for the beasts. Or even if your faith is rewarded, wouldn't you rather be free?' The smile vanishes from his face.

'I would never leave him,' he replies, and I feel the criticism like the smash of a body blow.

But then he looks at my face and smiles again, as if watching a small finch fly out of its gilded cage and up into the vastness of a dark blue sky.

'Besides,' he adds with an amused grin, 'I am his son!' With a happy shout, he catapults me up onto the horse's back, giving her a mighty slap on the rump. The black mare leaps and dances and finally dashes off down the desert road, away from the palace, her gallop as seamless as a silk ribbon. Far behind us, the manservant waves until I can no longer see him. With a thousand and one stars shining in the night sky, the smooth beating of my mare's hooves between my legs, and a diamond necklace clasped around my neck, I ride out into the world.

The End.

Acknowledgements

The Nights began as a series of diary entries way back in 2009. At the time I had recently separated from my husband and began keeping a journal as a way of managing the stress. I wrote at night, after putting my baby to bed, and soon began to identify with the famous story of Scheherazade, telling stories at night to stay alive.

The diary entries then became a novella that I turned into an artist's book, with help from artist Karen Smith and bookbinder Pamela Poluson. The book formed part of a touring exhibition I curated with Dr Caelli Jo Brooker. And it later became the bones of a Creative Writing PhD I completed at the University of Newcastle, under the supervision of Dr Caroline Webb.

Along the way, The Nights has been influenced by various writers and texts. First, and most obviously, ancient and modern versions of The 1001 Nights. Then Angela Carter's The Bloody Chamber, a breathtaking collection of erotic fairy tales; Cinthia Gannett's Gender and the Journal: Diaries and Academic Discourse; and Nikki Gemmell's The Bride Stripped Bare. I must also thank writer Nicola Hodder for the use of her Orange Moon haiku, and Bob Hass for permission to use his translation of Kobayashi Issa's haiku.

The Nights is available an audio book read by the brilliant London-based actor, Kelly Burke, with sound editing by Dan Baune of Noise Foundry Productions. Thank you to designers Mia Carter-Swain and Angus Hobba of Studio Zed at the University of Newcastle, with invaluable assistance from lecturer Carl Morgan, for their wonderful audio book cover design.

Many of the illustrations in this book are by emerging Hunter Valley designers, illustrators and artists: Abbey Hindmarch, Phoebe McMillan, Ashleigh Dibbs, Angus Hobba, Jacqueline Rheinburger, Jade Gallogly, Izzy Crerar, Joseph Matheson, Rachael Downey (Xenn) and Leanne Derring. Thanks to Lucy Jones for the book design, editor Shayanne Keats and publisher Bronwyn Mehan of Spineless Wonders.

I would like to thank Tony for his love and encouragement.

Meet the Author

Helen Hopcroft

Helen Hopcroft is a Tasmanian artist, performer, and writer. She holds a Royal College of Art MFA (Painting) and a Creative Writing PhD from Newcastle University.

Helen has written non-fiction books for the University of Newcastle and Hunter Valley Grammar School, with her publication list including The Australian, the Sydney Morning Herald, Art Monthly and The Griffith Review. Helen has been shortlisted for the 2022, 2023 and 2024 Newcastle Writers Festival/ Spineless Wonders joanne burns Microlit Award, and for the 2022 Nillumbik Prize for Contemporary Writing for her poem The Howling. Helen has been awarded a 2024 writer's residency at the Keesing Studio in Paris by Creative Australia (formerly Australia Council).'

Helen once spent a year dressed as Marie Antoinette for a piece of performance art titled 'My Year as a Fairy Tale'. She is currently writing a memoir about the experience. Helen lives in Maitland with her actor/musician husband Tony Jozef and daughter Sophie. She can be found online at www.helenhopcroft.com.

Meet the Narrator of The Nights Audio Book

Kelly Burke

Kelly Burke is a US/UK actor, writer, and activist. Her performance work has spanned the West End, Off-Broadway, and fringe and has included the solo play Zelda (Off-WestEnd finalist, Best Female Performer), Love for Sale (TimeOut New York Critics' Pick, Top 10 Things to See in NY). Screen work includes Marvel: Secret Invasion, FBI: International, Justice League, and Kill Your Friends. Kelly has won the AudioFile Earphones Award (2023) and has narrated 100+ audiobooks; she is thrilled to include 'The Nights' among them.

Meet the Designer

Lucy Jones

My journey into graphic design started young, and I've been in love with it ever since. Growing up with friends and family who were also passionate about creating and designing, I was naturally motivated and encouraged to pursue graphic design as a career.

Currently I am loving working within different areas in graphic design, such as publication design, visual identity and illustration. One aspect of graphic design that I have always loved is typography and this is reflected within my projects in the way that I creatively incorporate certain text or information.

Instagram: @lucyjjones.design
Portfolio: https://www.lucyjjones.com/
Contact: lucyjjones.design@gmail.com

Meet the Illustrators

Abbey Hindmarch

I adore visually realising ideas into unique images and graphics and aspire to grow as a designer in both animation and illustration by working on more projects in the future such as this one. It was such an honour to work collaboratively with so many talented individuals.

After recently graduating from my Bachelor's Degree in 2023 for Visual Communication Design, I am taking my first steps toward a career in the creative industries. I have been developing my own brand and hope to work with an animation company, whilst maintaining an online freelancing profile where I can also sell my own work.

Instagram: @abbey.demuredesigns
LinkedIn: https://www.linkedin.com/in/abbey-hindmarch-demure-designs/

Phoebe McMillan

I'm Phoebe and I like to do stuff. I'm a graphic designer where I mainly focus my passions in illustration, editorial work and print design plus many more. Currently pursuing my 3rd/4th year at Newcastle University and looking forward to freelancing and any other opportunities that may come.

Instagram: @Pheebs_Lea
Portfolio: https://phoebemcmillan.myportfolio.com/
Contact: phoebe.mcmillan2@gmail.com

Ash Dibbs

Based in Australia, Ash is a graphic designer specialising in brand design and print media. She is heavily influenced by grunge, surf and skate culture, and has found her unique voice in design. Ash has side passions of illustration, photography, and web design. Currently she is working as a freelance designer and building up the foundations of her future in design.

Instagram: @kingmamadesigns
Portfolio: ashleighdibbs.com
Contact: ashleighdibbsdesign@outlook.com

Angus Hobba

Angus is an animator and illustrator with a passion for mixed media and stop-motion animation. Much of Angus' work draws heavy influence from early web animation as well as classic horror films. At time of writing, he is a recent university graduate and is working on building out his body of work in animation as well as beginning production on a passion project short film.

Instagram: @Anguhs
Portfolio: Anguhscreative.com
Contact: angus.hobba@gmail.com

Jacqueline Rheinberger

I'm am currently studying a Bachelor of Visual Communication Design at the University of Newcastle, I love illustration and art is my biggest passion in life. Alongside illustration I do photography and other art forms, I'm excited to grow as a professional and start moving my career forward in the next coming years!

Instagram: @_jackys_art_
Contact: Jacky022799@gmail.com

Jade Gallogly

Jade Gallogly is a multi-disciplinary artist residing on Awabakal land, specializing in creating expressive, explosive and graphic work. Currently studying visual communication degree at the University of Newcastle and striving to become a notable and memorable creative in the vastly talented place of Newcastle.

Instagram: @stjadedesign
Contact: jadgaloogly@gmail.com

Izzy Crerar

Izzy Crerar is an up and coming designer and illustrator, exploring many aspects of the creative industry to create uniquely inspired work. Her work primarily consists of branding and illustrations and is currently building her portfolio, experience and skills. She draws much of her inspirations from other designers and artists of all types, bringing together her influences to synthesise a range of styles.

Instagram: @izzy.crerar
Portfolio: https://izzycrerar.myportfolio.com
Email: acviper27@gmail.com

Joseph Matheson

The Tiger Bride is an artwork showing the angelic beauty of the Tiger bride. The image itself is a little more pulled back then other artworks in this book and shows the beautiful transformation of a Tiger lady.

Instagram: @Barrel_of_goons
Contact: Josephmatheson74@gmail.com

Rachael Downey (Xenn)

Hello there, the name is Xenn. I'm a bubbling creative with a passionate mindset for the future of not just myself but the world around me. I am an aspiring digital designer with specialisations in graphic design, 3D design, UX/UI and Illustration. This project was an exceptional introduction to the industry and I'm looking forward to the future.

Currently I am a 2nd year student, graduating at the end of 2024. With high hopes for the future, I aspire to become a well-known designer for my wide range of skills within the industry to help land on my feet.

Instagram: @xennstudio
LinkedIn: https://www.linkedin.com/in/rachael-downey-0b1293260/
Contact: Xenn561@gmail.com

Leanne Deering

Leanne Deering lives in Newcastle Australia and is a Graphic Design Diploma graduate, Digital and Interactive Games Diploma graduate, currently doing a Bachelor of Visual Communication Design in Graphic Design and Illustration/Animation and Interaction Double Degree at the University of Newcastle to graduate in mid 2024 and has 6 years of experience working for a Children's TV Animation Production company in Administration and Graphic Design. Leanne loves to draw and always has a pencil and paper or a drawing tablet nearby ready to sketch out whatever fantastic ideas that spring to mind.

Portfolio: https://leedeedesigner.myportfolio.com/